6 $\frac{50}{m}$

"The Cat foraged tirelessly"

UNDERSTUDIES

Short Stories

By

MARY E. WILKINS

Author of
"Jerome" "Pembroke" "Madelon"
"Jane Field" etc.

ILLUSTRATED

NEW YORK AND LONDON

HARPER & BROTHERS PUBLISHERS

1901

CONTENTS

THE CAT

THE CAT

THE snow was falling, and the Cat's
fur was stiffly pointed with it, but he
was imperturbable. He sat crouched, ready
for the death-spring, as he had sat for hours.
It was night—but that made no difference—
all times were as one to the Cat when he was
in wait for prey. Then, too, he was under
no constraint of human will, for he was living alone that winter. Nowhere in the world
was any voice calling him; on no hearth
was there a waiting dish. He was quite
free except for his own desires, which tyran-
nized over him when unsatisfied as now.
The Cat was very hungry—almost fam-
ished, in fact. For days the weather had
been very bitter, and all the feebler wild
things which were his prey by inheritance,
the born serfs to his family, had kept, for
the most part, in their burrows and nests,
and the Cat's long hunt had availed him

3

nothing. But he waited with the inconceivable patience and persistency of his race; besides, he was certain. The Cat was a creature of absolute convictions, and his faith in his deductions never wavered. The rabbit had gone in there between those low-hung pine boughs. Now her little doorway had before it a shaggy curtain of snow, but in there she was. The Cat had seen her enter, so like a swift gray shadow that even his sharp and practised eyes had glanced back for the substance following, and then she was gone. So he sat down and waited, and he waited still in the white night, listening angrily to the north wind starting in the upper heights of the mountains with distant screams, then swelling into an awful crescendo of rage, and swooping down with furious white wings of snow like a flock of fierce eagles into the valleys and ravines. The Cat was on the side of a mountain, on a wooded terrace. Above him a few feet away towered the rock ascent as steep as the wall of a cathedral. The Cat had never climbed it—trees were the ladders to his heights of life. He had often looked with wonder at the rock, and miauled bitterly and resentfully as man does in the face of a forbidding

4

Providence. At his left was the sheer precipice. Behind him, with a short stretch of woody growth between, was the frozen perpendicular fall of a mountain stream. Before him was the way to his home. When the rabbit came out she was trapped; her little cloven feet could not scale such unbroken steeps. So the Cat waited. The place in which he was looked like a maelstrom of the wood. The tangle of trees and bushes clinging to the mountain-side with a stern clutch of roots, the prostrate trunks and branches, the vines embracing everything with strong knots and coils of growth, had a curious effect, as of things which had whirled for ages in a current of raging water, only it was not water, but wind, which had disposed everything in circling lines of yielding to its fiercest points of onset. And now over all this whirl of wood and rock and dead trunks and branches and vines descended the snow. It blew down like smoke over the rock-crest above; it stood in a gyrating column like some death-wraith of nature, on the level, then it broke over the edge of the precipice, and the Cat cowered before the fierce backward set of it. It was as if ice needles pricked his skin through his beautiful thick fur, but he never faltered and never once cried. He had nothing to gain from crying, and everything to lose; the rabbit would hear him cry and know he was waiting.

It grew darker and darker, with a strange white smother, instead of the natural blackness of night. It was a night of storm and death superadded to the night of nature. The mountains were all hidden, wrapped about, overawed, and tumultuously overborne by it, but in the midst of it waited, quite unconquered, this little, unswerving, living patience and power under a little coat of gray fur.

A fiercer blast swept over the rock, spun on one mighty foot of whirlwind athwart the level, then was over the precipice.

Then the Cat saw two eyes luminous with terror, frantic with the impulse of flight, he saw a little, quivering, dilating nose, he saw two pointing ears, and he kept still, with every one of his fine nerves and muscles strained like wires. Then the rabbit was out—there was one long line of incarnate flight and terror—and the Cat had her.

Then the Cat went home, trailing his prey through the snow.

THE CAT

The Cat lived in the house which his master had built, as rudely as a child's block-house, but stanchly enough. The snow was heavy on the low slant of its roof, but it would not settle under it. The two windows and the door were made fast, but the Cat knew a way in. Up a pine-tree behind the house he scuttled, though it was hard work with his heavy rabbit, and was in his little window under the eaves, then down through the trap to the room below, and on his master's bed with a spring and a great cry of triumph, rabbit and all. But his master was not there; he had been gone since early fall, and it was now February. He would not return until spring, for he was an old man, and the cruel cold of the mountains clutched at his vitals like a panther, and he had gone to the village to winter. The Cat had known for a long time that his master was gone, but his reasoning was always sequential and circuitous; always for him what had been would be, and the more easily for his marvellous waiting powers, so he always came home expecting to find his master.

When he saw that he was still gone, he dragged the rabbit off the rude couch which was the bed to the floor, put one little paw on the carcass to keep it steady, and began gnawing with head to one side to bring his strongest teeth to bear.

It was darker in the house than it had been in the wood, and the cold was as deadly, though not so fierce. If the Cat had not received his fur coat unquestioningly of Providence, he would have been thankful that he had it. It was a mottled gray, white on the face and breast, and thick as fur could grow.

The wind drove the snow on the windows with such force that it rattled like sleet, and the house trembled a little. Then all at once the Cat heard a noise, and stopped gnawing his rabbit and listened, his shining green eyes fixed upon a window. Then he heard a hoarse shout, a halloo of despair and entreaty; but he knew it was not his master come home, and he waited, one paw still on the rabbit. Then the halloo came again, and then the Cat answered. He said all that was essential quite plainly to his own comprehension. There was in his cry of response inquiry, information, warning, terror, and, finally, the offer of comradeship; but the man outside did not hear him, because of the howling of the storm.

Then there was a great battering pound at the door, then another, and another. The Cat dragged his rabbit under the bed. The blows came thicker and faster. It was a weak arm which gave them, but it was nerved by desperation. Finally the lock yielded, and the stranger came in. Then the Cat, peering from under the bed, blinked with a sudden light, and his green eyes narrowed. The stranger struck a match and looked about. The Cat saw a face wild and blue with hunger and cold, and a man who looked poorer and older than his poor old master, who was an outcast among men for his poverty and lowly mystery of antecedents; and he heard a muttered, unintelligible voicing of distress from the harsh, piteous mouth. There was in it both profanity and prayer, but the Cat knew nothing of that.

The stranger braced the door which he had forced, got some wood from the stock in the corner, and kindled a fire in the old stove as quickly as his half-frozen hands would allow. He shook so pitiably as he worked that the Cat under the bed felt the tremor of it. Then the man, who was small and feeble and marked with the scars of suffering which he had pulled down upon his own head, sat

down in one of the old chairs and crouched
over the fire as if it were the one love and desire of his soul, holding out his yellow hands
like yellow claws, and he groaned. The
Cat came out from under the bed and leaped
up on his lap with the rabbit. The man
gave a great shout and start of terror, and
sprang, and the Cat slid clawing to the floor,
and the rabbit fell inertly, and the man leaned,
gasping with fright, and ghastly, against the
wall. The Cat grabbed the rabbit by the
slack of its neck and dragged it to the man's
feet. Then he raised his shrill, insistent
cry, he arched his back high, his tail was a
splendid waving plume. He rubbed against
the man's feet, which were bursting out of
their torn shoes.

The man pushed the Cat away, gently
enough, and began searching about the little
cabin. He even climbed painfully the lad-
der to the loft, lit a match, and peered up in
the darkness with straining eyes. He feared
lest there might be a man, since there was a
cat. His experience with men had not been
pleasant, and neither had the experience of
men been pleasant with him. He was an
old wandering Ishmael among his kind;
he had stumbled upon the house of a broth-

er, and the brother was not at home, and he was glad.

He returned to the Cat, and stooped stiffly and stroked his back, which the animal arched like the spring of a bow.

Then he took up the rabbit and looked at it eagerly by the firelight. His jaws worked. He could almost have devoured it raw. He fumbled—the Cat close at his heels—around some rude shelves and a table, and found, with a grunt of self-gratulation, a lamp with oil in it. That he lighted; then he found a frying-pan and a knife, and skinned the rabbit, and prepared it for cooking, the Cat always at his feet.

When the odor of the cooking flesh filled the cabin, both the man and the Cat looked wolfish. The man turned the rabbit with one hand, and stooped to pat the Cat with the other. The Cat thought him a fine man. He loved him with all his heart, though he had known him such a short time, and though the man had a face both pitiful and sharply set at variance with the best of things.

It was a face with the grimy grizzle of age upon it, with fever hollows in the cheeks, and the memories of wrong in the dim eyes, but the Cat accepted the man unquestioning-

ly and loved him. When the rabbit was
half cooked, neither the man nor the Cat
could wait any longer. The man took it
from the fire, divided it exactly in halves,
gave the Cat one, and took the other himself. Then they ate.

Then the man blew out the light, called
the Cat to him, got on the bed, drew up the
ragged coverings, and fell asleep with the
Cat in his bosom.

The man was the Cat's guest all the rest
of the winter, and winter is long in the mountains. The rightful owner of the little hut
did not return until May. All that time the
Cat toiled hard, and he grew rather thin himself, for he shared everything except mice
with his guest; and sometimes game was
wary, and the fruit of the patience of days
was very little for two. The man was ill
and weak, however, and unable to eat much,
which was fortunate, since he could not hunt
for himself. All day long he lay on the
bed, or else sat crouched over the fire. It
was a good thing that fire-wood was ready
at hand for the picking up, not a stone's-
throw from the door, for that he had to attend to himself.

The Cat foraged tirelessly. Sometimes he

was gone for days together, and at first the man used to be terrified, thinking he would never return; then he would hear the familiar cry at the door, and stumble to his feet and let him in. Then the two would dine together, sharing equally; then the Cat would rest and purr, and finally sleep in the man's arms.

Towards spring the game grew plentiful; more wild little quarry were tempted out of their homes, in search of love as well as food. One day the Cat had luck—a rabbit, a partridge, and a mouse. He could not carry them all at once, but finally he had them together at the house door. Then he cried, but no one answered. All the mountain streams were loosened, and the air was full of the gurgle of many waters, occasionally pierced by a bird-whistle. The trees rustled with a new sound to the spring wind; there was a flush of rose and gold-green on the breasting surface of a distant mountain seen through an opening in the wood. The tips of the bushes were swollen and glistening red, and now and then there was a flower; but the Cat had nothing to do with flowers. He stood beside his booty at the house door, and cried and cried with his insistent triumph and complaint and pleading, but no one came to let him in. Then the Cat left his little treasures at the door, and went around to the back of the house to the pine-tree, and was up the trunk with a wild scramble, and in through his little window, and down through the trap to the room, and the man was gone.

The Cat cried again—that cry of the animal for human companionship which is one of the sad notes of the world; he looked in all the corners; he sprang to the chair at the window and looked out; but no one came. The man was gone, and he never came again.

The Cat ate his mouse out on the turf beside the house; the rabbit and the partridge he carried painfully into the house, but the man did not come to share them. Finally, in the course of a day or two, he ate them up himself; then he slept a long time on the bed, and when he waked the man was not there.

Then the Cat went forth to his hunting-grounds again, and came home at night with a plump bird, reasoning with his tireless persistency in expectancy that the man would be there; and there was a light in the

window, and when he cried his old master
opened the door and let him in.

His master had strong comradeship with
the Cat, but not affection. He never patted
him like that gentler outcast, but he had a
pride in him and an anxiety for his welfare,
though he had left him alone all winter without scruple. He feared lest some misfortune
might have come to the Cat, though he was
so large of his kind, and a mighty hunter.
Therefore, when he saw him at the door in all
the glory of his glossy winter coat, his white
breast and face shining like snow in the sun,
his own face lit up with welcome, and the Cat
embraced his feet with his sinuous body vibrant with rejoicing purrs.

The Cat had his bird to himself, for his master had his own supper already cooking on
the stove. After supper the Cat's master took
his pipe, and sought a small store of tobacco
which he had left in his hut over winter. He
had thought often of it; that and the Cat
seemed something to come home to in the
spring. But the tobacco was gone; not a
dust left. The man swore a little in a grim
monotone, which made the profanity lose its
customary effect. He had been, and was, a
hard drinker; he had knocked about the

world until the marks of its sharp corners were on his very soul, which was thereby calloused, until his very sensibility to loss was dulled. He was a very old man.

He searched for the tobacco with a sort of dull combativeness of persistency; then he stared with stupid wonder around the room. Suddenly many features struck him as being changed. Another stove-lid was broken; an old piece of carpet was tacked up over a window to keep out the cold; his fire-wood was gone. He looked, and there was no oil left in his can. He looked at the coverings on his bed; he took them up, and again he made that strange remonstrant noise in his throat. Then he looked again for his tobacco.

Finally he gave it up. He sat down beside the fire, for May in the mountains is cold; he held his empty pipe in his mouth, his rough forehead knitted, and he and the Cat looked at each other across that impassable barrier of silence which has been set between man and beast from the creation of the world.

THE MONKEY

THE MONKEY

THE monkey lived in his little den under the counter at the Bird-Fancier's. He was the only monkey there. It was a somewhat gloomy little shop, and the Monkey lived so far towards the back of it that he was seldom seen. Even the children did not often spy him out, and the most of their attention was concentrated upon the canaries, the parrots, the Angora cats, the white mice, and the rabbits. The canaries were more in evidence than the other inhabitants. The rabbits, of course, had nothing to say, and neither had the white mice. The parrots were either too sulky or desired exclusive stages for the exercise of their talents to say much. As for the Angora cats, they seemed cowed, possibly by their helplessness in the presence of such numbers of their natural prey. But the canaries were indomitable. Their wooden cages were small for their feathered bodies, but no bars could hold their songs, which floated in illimitable freedom forth into the city street. The Monkey seldom raised his voice at all. When he did, it had a curious effect. As a rule, people looked everywhere except at him for the source of it. It had a strange, far-off quality, perhaps from its natural assimilation with such widely different scenes. Of a right it belonged to the night chorus of a tropical jungle, and was a stray note from it, as out of place as anything could well be in this nearness to commonplaceness and civilization.

It was very dark in the Monkey's den. He peered out at every new sound, at every new step and voice, with his two yellow circles of eyes, which were bright with a curious blank brightness; they seemed not to have the recognition of intelligence until the object was within a certain distance.

The Monkey stayed for the greater part of his time in a swing fixed in the middle of his cage. He crouched thereon, folding his arms around the wires by which it was suspended. He crossed his hands upon his breast, and leaned his head forward in an attitude of contemplation. He might have been half asleep, and he might have been

sunken in a reverie. He looked like an epit-
ome of an Eastern sage. He might have
been on the home - stretch towards Nirvana
with that long wrinkle of thought over his
closed eyes, and that inscrutable, unsmiling
width of mouth, and unquestioning bend of
back.

The Bird-Fancier was something of a think-
er, and formed his own deductions from what
he saw. From living so long with these
little creatures below the staff, which never
met his questions with intelligible answers,
he had come to theorize. He was an old man
and not acquainted with books. He had
his own conception concerning the Monkey
and the rest, unwritten, but not unspoken
to a choice few.

One to whom he divulged his theories was
his old wife, who lived with him in the little
tenement over the shop; one was an old
woman cousin of hers, who lived with them
and worked for her board; and one was the
Boy. Not one of the three had the least understanding of anything which he said. If
it was in the daytime, the wife and the old
cousin went on with their work of cleaning
the bird - cages, and the Boy stood before
the Monkey's cage. If it was in the even-

ing, the old cousin knitted, for she was never idle, and the old wife dozed in her chair, and the Boy was of course not there, as he only stopped in the shop on his way to and from school. The Bird-Fancier had no more audience than if he had been himself an inhabitant of some distant jungle, and removed by force to a cage of civilization; but that did not disturb him at all. A true theorizer needs no sympathy unless he has an overweening conceit, and the Bird-Fancier was modest. He talked on, and never knew that he had no intelligent listeners. "Tell ye what it is," he would say, leaning back in his chair, with his eyes fixed as upon some far-off teacher, "I have thought it all out. It's simple enough when you know. You've all seen how berries and flowers run out. My brother Solomon, he had a beautiful strawberry-bed, berries as big as ducks' eggs, and the next year they had run out, not much bigger than pease. And my brother Solomon he had an asparagus-bed served him the same way; and you all know how pansies run out, till they get back to violets. All those little things in the shop are men and women run out. They ain't the beginning, as I have heard some say they believed, but they are the end. When a man dies, suppose he hasn't lived just the best kind of a life, but suppose he hasn't been wicked, not enough to be burned alive in fire and brimstone to all eternity, but suppose he ain't fitted to go into a higher sphere, suppose he wouldn't be happy there, let alone anything else; suppose he's just sort of no-account and little, not bad enough for hell, but not great enough for heaven, but there he is, and he's got to be somewhere. Well, souls that don't go straight to heaven or hell have got to go again into bodies; there ain't any keeping of them apart; might as well try to keep the three things that go to make up air apart. Into bodies those little souls have got to go, but they've got so much smaller through living no-account lives that they won't fit human bodies, so into the cats, and the birds, and the monkeys, and all the rest they go. They are folks run out. They are the end, or they will be when they finally die out, and all the animal races do. Take that Monkey. Just look at him. He's thousands of years old. He is just as likely as not one of the Bible Pharaohs run out. See him! When he looks up because he hears a noise, that noise brings back things to that Monkey that date from the foundation of the earth. There's what's left of something more'n you and I have ever known in that little head of his. Look at the way he uses his little hands! How did he learn to do that? I tell ye there is the key to Genesis and Revelation in that little Monkey, if anybody knew how to use it."

Perhaps because the Bird-Fancier regarded the Monkey in such philosophical fashion he did not care for him as a pet, but in fact he made pets of none of the little creatures in his shop. He regarded them all simply from a philosophical and financial point of view. He kept them well fed and clean, and sold them with alacrity whenever he was able. Then he forgot all about them. As for the old wife and the cousin, they were on a higher range of stupidity than the animals, and wondered at the other women who came into the shop and talked to the birds and cats as if they were children. They themselves would never have talked in such fashion to children.

So it happened that the Monkey had no real friend except the Boy. The Boy loved him with devotion, and he proved it. He saved every bit of his scanty pocket-money to buy delicacies for the Monkey—fruit and

loaf-sugar and peanuts. He was very fond
of sweets himself, and also of fruit, but he
seldom tasted any except when the Monkey
refused it. Then he ate it, and found it sweet
with the added sweet of generosity.

The Boy was a student at the high-school,
and not considered a promising one. In
fact, he lagged behind all his classes, and
had entered the school only after repeated
trials. He was a saturnine boy, with a face
not unlike the Monkey's own, with a curiously narrow height of forehead, and long
upper lip, and bright brown eyes. He had
outgrown his clothes, and his trousers and
jacket sleeves were too short, and he moved
with hitches of discomfort because of their
tightness. He came of a decent family, to
whom the unnecessary spending of money
was an unwritten prohibitory command-
ment. The father was a clerk on a small salary; there were two daughters, employed in
stores. The Boy had no mates among his
companions at school. He was as stupid
at sports as at lessons, and his saturninity
was against him.

The Boy's only pleasures and recreations
were his calls upon the Monkey at the Bird-
Fancier's shop. He stopped on his way to

and from school, and he usually secured a
few minutes at the noon intermission. He
would pass by the canaries and the parrots
and the rabbits, and he had a deeply rooted
aversion for the Angora cats. Straight to
the Monkey's little den he would go, crouch
down before it, and begin a curious, silent,
mouthing motion of his face. Then the Monkey would raise himself alertly, dart to the
side of his cage nearest the Boy, and respond
with an exactly similar motion. Now and
then he would reach out one little hairy hand
and it would cling around the Boy's fingers
like a baby's, and all the time the two kept
up that silent, mouthing communication,
which meant Heaven alone knew what to
the Monkey or the Boy. The Boy was the
only one whom the Monkey ever noticed in
such wise. No matter what were the blan-
dishments of any other visitor, he would do
no more than sit upon his swing, rub his
hands aimlessly, and stare over the visitor's
shoulder, as if he saw his shadow instead of
his personality. But for the Boy he always
made that lithe dart to the side of his cage,
and began that silent mouthing. The Boy
and the Monkey looked ridiculously alike at
those times, and the Bird-Fancier used to

eye them with shrewdness, but no mirth. Sometimes he told his nodding old wife and her industrious cousin in the evening that he believed that the Boy was kind of running out and proving his theory. Once he asked the Boy why he did not buy the Monkey; but the price was fifteen dollars, and the Boy could as soon have purchased an elephant.

One day the Boy brought a little looking-glass and fastened it to the side of the Monkey's cage. Some one had told him that monkeys were very cunning with looking-glasses; but the result was somewhat pathetic, and strengthened the Bird-Fancier in his theory. "He remembers the time when there was something at the back of the looking-glass, or he wouldn't act the way he does," he told his nodding wife and her illustrious cousin. The Monkey was wont to make a sudden dart at his reflection in the looking-glass, and stretch out both poor little arms past it in a piteous, futile effort of embrace. Then he would retreat forlornly to his perch. Sometimes the Boy got on the other side of the glass and grasped the little outreaching hands, and that seemed to satisfy the Monkey to a certain extent.

Towards night the Monkey became thoroughly alert. Life tingled in every nerve and muscle of his little hairy body. He was silent as ever, but he swung himself from end to end of his cage with curious doublings and undoublings. Doubled, he looked like a little man; undoubled, there was a sudden revelation of a beast. He clung to the wires; he revealed his chest, which was a beautiful blue color; the frown over his yellow eyes increased; he reached out for everything near his cage. If by any chance he could catch hold of anything, he was rejoiced.

He was never let out of his cage. He was a gentle monkey, but his owner had a perfect faith in his desire for mischief.

There was one superb black and white Angora cat which had the liberty of the shop and was not confined in a cage, and he used sometimes, though at a wary distance, to pass the Monkey's cell. Then the Monkey broke silence. He chattered with rage, he reached out a wiry little claw to incredible distances. Once he tweaked the cat's ear, and it fled, spitting. "That Monkey would kill the Cat if he got loose," said the Bird-Fancier, and the Monkey would indeed have been rejoiced to kill the Cat. He

would also have been rejoiced to kill some
of the other inhabitants of the shop, though
not so much because he hated them as because of the longing for destruction which
was in his blood. It was hard for a thing
used to the wild liberty of the jungle to be
kept in a little den under the counter of a
city shop. In the jungle he could at least
have torn leaves to shreds, he could have
swung from bough to bough, festooning
himself in wonderful leaping curves of life,
he could have killed those things which were
weaker than himself, or have fled chattering
with futile rage before those which were
stronger, or he could have died in unequal
combat. It would have been something to
have had the liberty of death. The deadly
monotony of his life wrought up the gentle
little creature to the point of madness when
night came on. He was, as it were, choking
for liberty. He glared forth at the canaries
and the rabbits, he showed all his teeth at the
Bird-Fancier when the old man gave him
the banana which was his nightly meal,
and clutched it through the wires with vicious
greed. Then he would tear off the rind, and
so doing catch a glimpse of the monkey in
the looking-glass, and drop his supper, and

spring for him, and reach out those pathetic little empty arms.

"He is the gentlest monkey I ever saw," said the Bird-Fancier; "but for all that, I wouldn't let him loose in the shop."

The Bird-Fancier had owned the Monkey about a year, when one night, through some oversight, the cage door was left unfastened, and the Monkey escaped. He worked at the catch for a long time, and at last it yielded, and he was free.

It was about two o'clock in the morning, and the full moonlight lay in the shop, and besides that was the white glare of electricity from across the street. It was so light that occasionally a canary thought it was day and woke and chirped, and the parrots stirred uneasily, and shrieked or laughed.

The Monkey slipped out of his cage, and the greatest joy which he had ever known was upon him. He was a vibration of liberty; not a nerve in his little body but thrilled with the utmost delight of life and freedom. He went about the shop with long lopes. He did not look so much like a little man as like a beast. The beautiful black and white Angora cat was sleeping peacefully on top of the white-mice cage, and the Monkey

spied him, and made one leap for his back.
Then he rode him furiously around the shop,
winding his wiry arms in a strangling embrace around his neck, but the Cat escaped
by a wild plunge through the window, and
the Monkey slid off. He could have followed,
but he had other things to attend to. He
flew at a little golden ball of sleeping canary
in his tiny cage, then at another, and another,
then at the gold-fishes. The parrots he let
alone, after he had shrewdly eyed their hooked
beaks. He had thoughts of the rabbits which
stood aloof in their cages with dilated pink
eyes of terror, and supplicating hang of paws,
and quivering nostrils, but they were as large
as the Monkey, and he had no knowledge as
to their powers of defence; besides, he could
not easily get at them. But he loved to pull
the gold-fishes out of their crystal bowls
and watch them gasp on the floor, and
he enjoyed the flutterings of the canary-
birds.

It was quite a long time before the cousin
up-stairs awoke. She woke first, because she
was the lightest sleeper. Then she spoke
to the Bird-Fancier, and told him that something was wrong in the shop, and all three
hurried down, thinking it was fire. But

it was only a little spark of liberty let loose to work its own will.

The Monkey had wrought considerable destruction; several canaries would never trill again, and a number of gold-fishes lay strewn about the floor. The Bird-Fancier whipped the Monkey back to his cage, and fastened the door, and the little animal caught sight of his reflection in the looking-glass and darted towards it with outstretched arms.

"That Monkey has destroyed more than he is worth," the Bird-Fancier told his wife and her cousin. "There is no profit in keeping monkeys."

The next morning he gave the Monkey his breakfast as usual, and said nothing by way of reproach, being alive to the absurd futility of it. But he looked at him, and the Monkey showed all his teeth, and clutched his little dish of bread and milk and flung it on the floor of his den.

When the Boy came in on his way to school the Bird-Fancier, contrary to his custom, waxed loquacious. He pointed to the bodies of the dead canaries and the gold-fishes. "See what your Monkey has done in the night," he said.

THE MONKEY

The Boy looked soberly at the dead birds and the fishes, then at the man.

"He has killed more than he is worth," said the Bird-Fancier.

Then the cousin, who was cleaning the cage of one of the dead canaries, piped up in a slender, shrill voice, not unlike a bird's: "Yes, only see! And if I hadn't woke just as I did, he would have killed the whole shopful. Better leave monkeys in their woods where they belong."

The Boy looked from one to the other, but he said nothing. Then he went as usual to the Monkey's den, and the Monkey came to the side of it, and the two mouthed at each other silently with perfect understanding. When the Boy was leaving the shop the Bird-Fancier stopped him. He had been having a whispered consultation with his wife.

"See here," he said; "if you want that Monkey, you can have him." The Boy turned pale and stared at him. "I will put him in an old parrot-cage," said the Bird-Fancier, "and you can stop and get him this noon."

"For nothing?" gasped the Boy.

"Yes, for nothing," replied the Bird-Fancier. "I am tired of keeping him. Monkeys ain't very salable."

"For nothing?" repeated the Boy.

"Yes, you needn't pay a cent," said the Bird-Fancier, looking at him curiously.

Such an expression of rapture came into the Boy's face that it was fairly glorified. It was broadened with smiles until it looked cherubic. His brown eyes were like stars.

"Thank you," he stammered, for he was at that time of life when he was ashamed of saying thank you. Then he went out, and to school, and for the first time in months learned his lessons with no effort, and seemed to see truths clearly, and not through a fog. He had a great happiness to live up to, and for some minds happiness is the only dispeller of fogs; the Boy's was of that sort.

After school he ran all the way home to make sure that the Monkey would be welcome, and that his mother would not refuse him shelter, then he went without his dinner to fetch him.

When the Boy arrived at the Bird-Fancier's the Monkey was all ready to depart, ensconced in the old parrot-cage. The Boy went out of the store, dragged to one side with the weight of his precious burden, and

34

"*The Bird-Fancier watched him*"

for the first time in his life the ecstasy of possession was upon him. He had never fairly
known that he was alive until he had come
into the ownership of this tiny life of love.

The Bird-Fancier watched him going down
the street, and turned to his wife, who was
stroking the Angora cat, and the cousin,
who was feeding a canary which had just
arrived. The Boy, going down the street,
had his face bent over the Monkey, and the
two were mouthing to each other. "I am
right, you may depend upon it," he said.
"There goes one monkey carrying another."

THE SQUIRREL

THE SQUIRREL

THE Squirrel lived with his life-long mate near the farm-house. He considered himself very rich, because he owned an English walnut-tree. Neither he nor his mate had the least doubt that it belonged to them and not to the Farmer. There were not many like it in the State or the whole country. It was a beautiful tree, with a mighty spread of branches full of gnarled strength. Nearly every year there was a goodly promise of nuts, which never came to anything, so far as the people in the farm-house were concerned. Every summer they looked hopefully at the laden branches, and said to each other, " This year we shall have nuts," but there were never any. They could not understand it. But they were old people; had there been boys in the family, it might have been different. Probably they would have solved the mystery. It was simple enough. The Squirrel and his mate considered the nuts as theirs, and appropriated them. They loved nuts; they were their natural sustenance; and through having an unquestioning, though unwitting, belief in Providence, they considered that nuts which grew within their reach were placed there for them as a matter of course. There were the Squirrels, and there were the nuts. No nuts, no Squirrels. The conclusion was obvious to such simple intelligences.

As soon as the nuts were ripe the Squirrel and his mate were busy all day, gathering the nuts, and then carrying them to their little storehouse under the wood-pile. Back and forth they sped with such smooth swiftness that it was no more perceptible than the passing of a beam of light.

The Squirrels were very near the color tones of the tree, which, moreover, held its leaves late; only a boy would have been likely to spy them out.

"It is a strange thing about those nuts," the Farmer's Wife often said to her husband, peering up at the tree with her dim old eyes, and he assented. The old couple were given to sitting out on their porch after supper as long as the evenings were warm enough, and it was a late autumn that year. There were occasional frosts, but summer-like days between.

The Farmer and his Wife were a fond old couple. They had never had any children, and the sympathy of their own natures had drawn them more closely together through the long years. They looked and thought alike. If anything, the Wife had the stronger nature of the two, but both of them were gentle, yet with a certain wariness and shrewdness, not unlike that of the Squirrels. They were very careful of their money, and saved every penny, and had made considerable provision for their old age. They looked forward to nothing except perfect peace and comfort on this earth for the rest of their lives, and as for what would come after—they had a religious hope.

They had always looked at their English walnut-tree and speculated as to what could have become of the nuts, but the speculation did not disturb them at all. They took things which had happened for some time easily, being gently conservative to the bone. "Seems as if them nuts must drop off that tree and be picked up," said the Farmer, "but there ain't no boys."

"No, there ain't no boys," said his Wife.

Sometimes the Farmer used to walk about under the tree and look on the ground for fallen nuts, and his Wife did likewise, but they never found any. They were not aware of four of the keenest eyes of watchfulness and wariness in the whole world intent upon them from some corner of hiding. Now and then they saw one of the Squirrels slipping along the stone wall, and looked at him with that interest which always attaches to a Squirrel, perhaps because the swiftness of his passing from observation gives him a certain rarity and preciousness. Sometimes the Farmer's Wife observed one sitting upright on the wall, holding a nut in his forepaws and nibbling at it boldly. "Maybe he has got one of our walnuts," said she.

"He couldn't get the whole treeful," said the Farmer.

"No, he couldn't," assented the Wife.

The capacity of the Squirrels for excelling in their given walk of life was as much of a secret to them as was theirs to the Squirrels.

It was in the bright, clear morning that they oftenest caught glimpses of the Squirrels, for the morning was their period of fullest life and activity. Then, when the smell of passing leaves and ripened fruit was in the air, and the grass was white and crisp with something between frost and dew, did the Squirrels feel their joy of life to the utmost. They darted hither and yon, mostly unobserved, since they could fairly outspeed human observation. Not a nut that fell from the tree escaped them. They went to and fro between the tree and their hoard under the wood-pile. They were very rich indeed. That year there had been nearly a bushel of nuts on the English walnut-tree, and they garnered them all. The same delight in their providence, and sense of self-gratulation, and security as to the future, were over them as over the old couple in the farm-house. They too looked forward to peace and comfort on earth; as for the unknown future, they did not dream it existed. They had no religious hope, but their utter lack of questioning made them too trustful for any anxiety. They had no premonitions of a future stage when there might be no stone walls for running along, and no nut-trees, and yet Squirrels. Their needs and their supplies were entireties not to be separated by any conception of theirs.

When they had garnered every nut from

the English walnut-tree they were indeed an opulent pair. They were, of course, acquainted with other Squirrels, but none of them approached themselves in point of richness. None of the others had English walnuts, and none had such a plentiful store. They looked forward to a winter of fatness and luxury and love, for the two little creatures loved each other as faithfully as did the old couple in the farm-house. None of the other Squirrels knew of their hiding-place under the wood-pile, nobody had discovered the cunning passage which led to it. It was the last of October, and they felt perfectly secure. They had reached that point, so seldom reached by either Men or Squirrels, when care as to material things is over. Then came the day of their downfall.

The Farmer's Wife thought that the wood-pile should be taken down, and the wood split and stored in the shed before winter set in, and the Farmer obediently began the task. It was not a large pile, and he was too thrifty to hire help. He chopped away patiently day after day, but it was a long time before the Squirrels fairly took alarm for the safety of their store. They had grown to believe in its impregnability, and the impregnability

"They chattered angrily"

of their right of possession. They kept out of the way while the old man was at work, scampering in the autumn woods, enjoying themselves, and always with the thought of their bountiful provision for the future in mind.

At last they began to grow anxious. They hung aloof and chattered angrily. They sat on the stone wall with great tails arching over their backs, so near that the gentle old man thought they must be growing tame, and at last the blow fell.

One morning the Farmer discovered the Squirrels' hoard. He went into the house and told his Wife. "What d'ye think?" he said. "It was them Squirrels that have stole all them English walnuts."

"You don't say so!" said she.

"Yes, they have. There's nigh a bushel of them under the wood-pile."

"You don't say so!" said she again.

The old couple went out together and looked at the winter hoard of the other couple.

"Well," said the Farmer's Wife, "you'll have to get the bushel basket and pick them up and bring them into the house, and spread them out on the garret floor. It's the first time we've ever had any nuts off that tree.

I declare, them Squirrels have been stealing them all this time!"

The old man hesitated. He was as thrifty as his Wife, and had as great a pleasure in possessions, but he had more points of view. "Seems kind of too bad when they've worked so hard," he remarked.

"Why is it too bad? Ain't they our nuts?" said his Wife, with wonder in her soft eyes. "They've stole our nuts."

"Well," said the old man.

He got the bushel basket and gathered up the nuts. There was distracted, but wary, comment from the Squirrels. They skirmished about or the stone wall, and watched this run upon their little bank with unavailing chatters of protest. At this time, if they had had faith, they might have lost it. At the beginning of winter the Squirrel and his mate, no longer young, were thrown upon the world penniless, and all their season's labor was lost.

When the nuts were all heaped up on the garret floor the old man and his Wife looked at them. The old man was still doubtful. "It seems most too bad, when they've worked so hard, don't it?" he said, with a break in his voice.

" Ain't they our nuts, and didn't they steal them?" returned his Wife. She was as kindly as her husband, except when it came to questions of sheer justice; then she was pitiless.

But the old man was still anxious. All that day he had an eye upon the frenzied Squirrels darting hither and thither along the wall, with occasional peeps of unbelief that the worst was true, at their violated storehouse. That night he went down to the village store and purchased a bushel of shagbarks, and brought them home, leaning painfully to one side with their weight. He stole out to the wood-pile, all unseen by his Wife, and deposited them in the Squirrels' hiding-place. The next day, and several days after that, he had an attack of rheumatism and was unable to chop wood.

Then a light snow came, the first of the season, and he said to his Wife that he didn't know but it might be just as well to leave the rest of that wood-pile for a while, seeing as he was so lame in his joints and the wood was so wet, and the shed nigh about full anyway. And she assented, saying that she guessed there was about enough wood in the shed to last till spring, and she didn't want him to get any more cold, and it cost so much to hire help. She suspected nothing about the shagbarks and the Squirrels, and the old man did not tell her, though he felt guilty. He had never been in the habit of concealing anything from his faithful old helpmeet, not even his good deeds. But there are some deeds which are too intimate with one's self and God for even the listening ear of human love, and too much a part of the soul for even wedlock to unveil. Then, too, the old man was afraid that his Wife would think that he had been extravagant.

That winter the Farmer used often to gaze out of the window from behind his Wife's blooming row of geraniums, and think with a sensation which was like a warmth in his soul how the Squirrels were supplied with plenty for their needs until spring. But he crept out one day when his Wife was away and investigated, and not a nut was in the storehouse. He straightened his rheumatic back painfully and stared at the little empty cellar. Then the chatter of a Squirrel struck his dull ears. He looked for a long time, and finally spied him sitting on the stone wall, eying him with the wariest eyes of incipient motion, his tail already stiffened for flight.

48

"Wonder if that's one of 'em?" thought the old man. He could not know that the Squirrel and his mate had moved all their new store of nuts to another hiding-place in the woods at the foot of a birch-tree, because they were filled with suspicion and distrust of him. His restitution was nothing. What were shagbarks to English walnuts? They were of an inferior quality anyway, and how did they alter the fact of the appropriation of the others?

The gentle old man whistled. "Be you the thief?" he asked.

Then the Squirrel began to chatter fiercely at the Farmer, though he was always ready to fly at his slightest motion. The frosty air seemed to fairly shiver and shake with that tiny volley of accusation. There was the thief who had stolen the store which had been provided for himself and his mate by the Providence which had created them. There was the thief who had sinned doubly, both against them and that Providence which had shaped both their need and their supply.

Finally the old man went back to his house, and the Squirrel slipped swiftly away along the stone wall towards his secret dwelling.

When the Farmer's Wife returned, she proposed cracking some of the English walnuts. "They must be dry enough now," she said. So the old man brought down some from the garret, and fell to work. "I dun'no' as I want any," he remarked, as he pounded. "I never did care much about nuts anyway, and somehow I've always felt as if we'd stole the Squirrels' after they'd worked so hard."

"How silly you be!" said his Wife, but she looked at him lovingly. "You were always too tender-hearted for your own good. Talk about stealing, it was the Squirrels that stole our nuts."

But the Squirrel and his mate, whose ancestors had held the whole land, and the fruit thereof, in feudal tenure to the Creator of it all, since the beginning of things, had different views. They were in the woods champing their supper of shagbarks, and often finding a wormy one, and they considered that the Farmer had stolen their nuts.

THE LOST DOG

THE LOST DOG

THE dog was speeding, nose to the ground; he had missed his master early in the morning; now it was late afternoon, but at last he thought he was on his track. He went like a wind, his ears pointed ahead, his slender legs seemingly flat against his body; he was eagerness expressed by a straight line of impetuous motion. He had had nothing to eat all day; he was spent with anxiety and fatigue and hunger; but now, now, he believed he was on his master's track, and all that was forgotten.

But all at once he stopped, his tail dropped between his legs, and he skulked away from the false track in an agony of mortification and despair. It had ended abruptly at a street corner, where the man had taken a carriage. He doubled and went back for his life to the last place where he had seen his master in the morning. It was a crowded corner, and the people were passing and repassing, weaving in and out, a great concourse of humanity following the wonderful maze of their own purposes.

The dog sniffed at the heels of one and another. He followed and retreated; he dodged and skulked. He was a thing of abject apology, and felt no resentment at a kick when he got in the way of that tide of human progress. The dog without his master was like modesty without raiment, like a body without a soul. Without his master he was not even a dog; he was a wandering intelligence only, and had fallen below his inheritance of dog-wit.

He yelped now and then, but his yelp would have been unintelligible to another of his species. He put his nose to the ground; the confusion of scents and his despair made him, as it were, deaf in his special acuteness. He blindly ran after this one and that one. Now and then he heard a voice which made his heart leap, and was after the owner at a bound, but it was never his master.

The city lights were blazing out and the raw night settling down; on the corner were two steady interweaving streams to the right and left of people going homeward, and all with the thought of shelter and food and fire and rest.

Finally the dog fastened his despairing eyes upon a man coming around the corner, and he followed him. He knew he was not his master, but there was that about him which awakened that wisdom of dependence which had come down to him through generations. He knew that here was a man who could love a dog.

So he followed him on and on, moving swiftly at heel, keeping well in shadow, his eyes fixed anxiously upon the man's back, ready to be off at the first symptom of his turning. But the man did not see him until he had reached his home, which was a mile beyond the city limits, quite in the country.

He went up to a solitary house set in a deep yard behind some fir-trees. There were no lights in the windows. The man drew a key from his pocket and unlocked the door. Then he saw the dog.

He looked hard at the dog, and the dog looked piteously at him. The dog wagged his tail in frantic circles of conciliation. The full moon was up, and there was a street-lamp, so the two could see each other quite distinctly. Both the dog and the man were thoroughbreds. The dog saw a man, young, in shabby clothes, which he wore like a gentleman, with a dark and clear-cut face. The man saw a dog in a splendid suit of tawny gold hair, with the completeness of his pure blood in every line and curve of his body. The man whistled; the dog pressed closer to him; his eyes upon his face were like a woman's. The man stopped and patted the dog on his tawny gold head, then entered the house and whistled again, and the dog followed him in.

That evening the dog lay on an old skin rug before the hearth-fire, but uneasily, for his new master was doing something which disturbed him. He was singing with a magnificent tenor voice, and the dog was vaguely injured in his sensibilities by music. At first he howled, but, when the man bade him be quiet, he protested no longer, except for an occasional uneasy roll of an eye or twitch of an ear at a new phrase.

The dog had had a good supper; he had eaten rather more than the man. There was plenty of wood on the hearth, though the reserve was not large. But the man who sang had the optimism of a brave soul which, when it is striving to its utmost, can-

"Both the dog and the man were thoroughbreds"

not face the image of defeat without a feeling of disgrace.

He was a great singer; he had been born to it, and he had worked for it. Some day the material fruits of it—the milk and honey of prosperity—would be his; in the meantime there was his voice and his piano; and while there was wood, let his hearth-fire blaze merrily; and while he had a crust, let him share it with a dog that was needy.

Now and then the man in the intervals of his singing patted the dog, and spoke to him caressingly; and the dog looked at him with a gratitude which reached immensity through its unspeakableness.

The dog wore no collar, and the man marvelled at that.

It was midnight when there came a step at the door and a ring, and the dog was on his feet with a volley of barks. He was ready to charge a whole army for the sake of this man whom he had known only a few hours. But in this case he would have attacked, not an enemy who threatened his master's safety, but a friend who brought him wealth and fame.

When the man returned to the room with the out-of-doors cold clinging to him, his face was radiant, jubilant. The tenor who had been singing in the opera-house had broken his engagement, and the manager had come for him.

He told the dog, for lack of another companion, and the dog reared himself on two legs, like a man, in his ecstasy of joyful comradeship, and placed his paws on the man's shoulders and licked his young face. Then the man sat down at his piano, and sang over and over his part in the opera, and the dog gave only one low howl under his breath, then lay down on the skin rug, with twitching ears and back.

That night the man's golden age began, and the dog shared it. His new master had his share of superstition, and regarded the old saying that a dog following one brought luck, and had, besides his love for the animal, a species of gratitude and sense of obligation.

In the days of luxurious living which followed, the dog was to the front with the man. He rode with him in his softly cushioned carriage to the opera-house, and slept in his dressing-room while the music and the applause went on. Occasionally he would make a faint protesting howl when a loud strain reached his ears. The dog loved the man for love's sake alone; that which won the adulation of men was his trial. He loved him, not for his genius, but in spite of it.

The dog in this new life grew to his full possibility of beauty and strength. His coat shone like satin; he was a radiant outcome of appreciation and good food; but palmier days still were to come.

One day the tenor brought home a wife; then the dog for the first time knew what it was to be the pet of a woman. Then he wore a great bow of blue satin on his silver collar, and often his coat smelled of violets.

The new wife was adorable; the touch of her little soft hands on the dog's head was ecstasy; and *she* did not sing, but talked to him, and praised him with such sweet flattery that he used to roll his eyes at her like a lover, and thrust an appealing paw upon her silken lap.

Then he grew to an appreciation of himself; all his abjectness vanished. He became sure of himself and of love. He was a happy dog except for one thing. Always in his sleep he searched for his old lost master. He was never on the street but down went his nose to the ground for the scent of those old footsteps.

And one day, when he had been with his new friends two years, he found him. His mistress's carriage was waiting, and he beside it, one day in spring when they were selling daffodils and violets on the street, and doves were murmuring around the church towers, and the sparrows clamorous, and everything which had life, in which hope was not quite dead, was flying, and darting, and blossoming, and creeping out into the sunlight.

Then the dog saw his old master coming down the street, scraping the pavement with his heavy feet—an old man, mean and meanly clad, with no grace of body or soul, unless it might have been the memory of, and regret for, the dog. Him he had loved after the best fashion which he knew. This splendid brute thing, with his unquestioning devotion, had kept alive in him his piteous remnant of respect for self, and had been to him more than any one of his own kind, who had put him to shame, and sunk him in the lowest depths of ignominy by forcing his realization of it.

The dog stood still, with ears erect and tail stiff, then was after his old master with a mighty bound. At first the man cursed and kicked at him, then looked again and swore 'twas his old dog, and stroked his head with that yellow clutch of avarice for his own possession and his own profit, rather than affection, which was the best his poor soul could compass.

But the dog followed him, faithful not only to his old master, but to a nobler thing, the faithfulness which was in himself—and maybe by so doing gained another level in the spiritual evolution of his race.

THE PARROT

THE PARROT

THE parrot was a superb bird — a vociferous symmetry of green and gold and ruby red, with eyes like jewels, with their identical irresponsibility of fire, with a cling, not of loving dependence, but of ruthless insistence, to his mistress's hand, or the wires of his cage, and a beak of such a fine curve of cruelty as was never excelled.

The parrot's mistress was a New England woman, with the influence of a stern training strong upon her, and yet with a rampant force of individuality constantly at war with it. She lived alone, except for the parrot, in a sharply angled village house, looking upon the world with a clean, repellent glare of windows and white broadside of wall, in a yard whose grass seemed as if combed always by one wind, so evenly slanted was it. There was a decorously trimmed rosebush on either side of the front door, and one elm-tree at the gate which leaned decidedly to the south with all its green sweep of branches, and always in consequence gave the woman a vague and unreasoning sense of immorality.

Inside, the house showed stiff parallelograms of white curtains, and dull carpets threadbare with cleanliness, and little pools of reflected light from the polished surfaces of old tables and desks, and one glass-doored bookcase filled with works on divinity bound uniformly in rusty black.

The woman's father had been a Congregational clergyman, and this was his old library. She had read every book over and over with a painful concentration, and afterwards admitted her crime of light-mindedness, and prayed to be forgiven, and have her soul so wrought upon by grace that she might truthfully enjoy these godly publications. She had never read a novel; she looked upon cards as wiles of the devil; once, and once only, had she been to a concert of strictly secular music in the town-hall, and had felt thereby contaminated for days, having a temperament which was strangely wrought upon by music, and yet a total ignorance of it. She felt guilty under the

influence of all harmonies which did not,
through being linked to spiritual words, turn
her soul to thoughts of heaven; and yet
sometimes, to her sore bewilderment, the
tunes which she heard in church did not so
sway her wayward fancy; and then she ac-
cused herself of being perverted in her comprehension of good through the influence
of that worldly concert.

. This woman went nowhere except to
church, to prayer-meeting, to the village
store, and once a month to the missionary
sewing-circle, and to the supper and sociable
in the evening. She dressed always in black,
her face was delicately spare, her lips were
a compressed line of red, and yet she was
pretty, with a prettiness almost of youth,
from that undiminished fire of the spirit
which dwelt within her, as securely caged
by her training and narrowness of life as
was the parrot by the strong wires of his
house.

The parrot was the one bright thing in
the woman's life; he was the link with that
which was outside her, and yet with that
which was of her truest inwardness of self.
This tropical thing, screaming and laughing, and shrieking out dissonant words, and

oftentimes speeches, with a seemingly diabolical comprehension of the situation, was the one note of utter freedom and irresponsibility in her life. She adored him, but always with a sense of guilt upon her. Often she said to herself that some judgment would come upon her for so loving such a bird, for there was in truth about him as much utter gracelessness as can be conceived of in one of the lower creation. He swore such oaths that his mistress would fairly fly out of the door with hands to her ears. Always, when she saw a caller coming, she would remove his cage to a distant room and shut all the doors between. She felt that if any one heard him sending forth those profane shrieks, possibly to his spiritual contamination, she might be driven by her sense of duty to have the bird put to death. She knew, as she believed, that she risked her own soul by listening and yet loving, but that she had no courage to forego.

As for the parrot, he loved his mistress, if he loved anything. He would extend an ingratiating but deceitful claw towards her between his cage wires whenever she approached. If ever she had a torn finger in consequence, she made light of it, like any

wound of love. He would take morsels of
food from between her thin lips.

When she talked to him with that language of love which every soul knows by instinct, and which is intelligible to all who
are not too deadened and deafened with self,
he would cock his glittering head and look
at her with that inscrutable jewel-eye of his.
Then he would thrust out a claw towards
her with that insistence which was ruthless,
and yet not more ruthless than the insistence
of love, and often say something which con-
founded her with its apparent wisdom of
sequence, and then the doubt and the conviction which at once tormented and en-
raptured her would seize upon her.

She tried to conceal it from herself, she
held it as the rankest atheism, she thought
vaguely of the idols of wood and stone in
the hymn-book, of Baal, and the golden calf,
and the witch of Endor, and every forbidden thing which is the antithesis of holiness,
and yet she could not be sure that her parrot
had not a soul. Sometimes she wondered
if she ought to speak of her state of mind
to the minister, and ask his advice, but she
shrank from doing that, both because of her
natural reserve and because he was unmar-

ried, and she knew that people had coupled his name with hers. He was of suitable age, and it was urged that a match for him with the solitary daughter of the former minister would be eminently appropriate.

The woman had never considered the possibility of such a thing, although she had heard of the plan of the parish from many a female friend. She had had her stifled dreams in her early youth, but she had not been one to attract lovers, being perchance bound as to her true graces somewhat too much after the fashion of her father's old divinity books. No man in her whole life had ever looked at her with a look of love, and she had never heard the involuntary break of it in his voice. Sometimes on summer evenings, she, sitting by her open window, saw village lovers going past with covert arms of affection around slim, girlish waists. One night she saw, half shrinking from the sight, a fond pair standing in the shadow of the elm-tree at her gate, and clasped in each other's arms, and saw the girl's face raised to the young man's for his eager kisses, the while a murmur of love, like a song in an unknown tongue, came to her ears.

It was a warm night, and the parrot's cage

was slung for coolness on a peg over the window, and he shrieked out, with his seemingly unholy apprehension of things, "What is that? What is that? Do you know what that is, Martha?" Then ended his query with such a wild clamor of laughter that the lovers at the gate fled, and his mistress, Martha, rose and took the bird in.

She set him on the sitting-room table along with the Bible and the Concordance, and a neat little pile of religious papers, while she lighted a lamp. Then she looked half affrightedly, half with loving admiration, at the gorgeous thing, swinging himself frantically on the ring in his cage.

Then, swifter than lightning, down on his perch he dropped, cast a knowing eye like a golden spark at the solitary woman, and shrieked out again:

"What was that? What was that, Martha? Martha, Martha, Martha, Martha. Polly don't want a cracker; Polly don't want a cracker; Polly will be damned if she eats a cracker. You don't want a cracker, do you, Martha? Martha, Martha, Martha, want a cracker? What was that, Martha? Martha, want a cracker? Martha will be damned if she eats a cracker. Martha, Martha, Martha!"

Then the bird was off in such another explosion of laughs, thrusting a claw through his wires at his mistress, that the house rang with them. Martha took the extended claw tenderly; she put her pretty, delicate, faded face to that treacherous beak; she murmured fond words. Then ceased suddenly as she heard a step on the walk, and the parrot cried out, with a cry of sharpest and most sardonic exultation:

"He's coming, he's coming, Martha!"

Then, to Martha's utter horror, before she had time to remove the bird, a knock came on her front door, which stood open, and there was the minister.

He had called upon her before, in accordance with his pastoral duty, but seldom, and always with his mother, who kept his house with him. This time he was alone, and there was something new in his manner.

He was a handsome man, no younger than she, but looking younger, with a dash of manner which many considered unministerial. He would not allow Martha to remove the parrot, though she strove tremblingly to do so, and laughed with a loud peal like a boy when the parrot shrieked, to his mistress's sore discomfiture:

"'He's coming, Martha'"

THE PARROT

"He's come, Martha, damned if he ain't. Martha, Martha, where in hell is that old cracker?"

Martha felt as if her hour of retribution had come, and she was vaguely and guiltily pleased and relieved when the minister not only did not seem shocked with the free speaking of her bird, but was apparently amused.

She watched him touch the parrot caressingly, and heard him talk persuasively, coaxing him to further speech, and for the first time in her life a complete sense of human comradeship came to her.

After a while the parrot resolved himself into a gorgeous plumy ball of slumber on his perch, then his mistress sat an hour in the moonlight with the minister.

She had put out the lamp at his request, timidly, and yet with a conviction that such a course must be strictly proper, since it was proposed by the minister.

The two sat near each other at the open window, and the soft sweetness of the summer night came in, and the influence of the moonlight was over them both. The lovers continued to stroll past the gate, and a rule of sequence holds good in all things. Presently, for the first time in her life, this solitary woman felt a man's hand clasping her own little slender one in her black cashmere lap. The minister made no declaration of love in words, but the tones of his voice were enough.

When he spoke of exchanging with a neighboring clergyman in two weeks, the speech was set to the melody of a love-song, and there was no cheating ears which were attuned to it, no matter if it had been long in coming.

When the minister took his leave, and Martha lighted her lamp again, the parrot stirred and woke, and brought that round golden eye of his to bear upon her face flushed like a girl's, and cried out:

"Why, Martha! why, Martha! what is the matter?"

Then Martha dropped on her knees beside the cage, and touched the bird's head with a finger of tenderest caressing.

"Oh, you darling, you darling, you precious!" she murmured, and began to weep. And the parrot did not laugh, but continued to eye her.

"He has come, hasn't he, Martha?" said he.

Then Martha was more than ever inclined

"' Why, Martha!   What is the matter?'"

to think that the bird had a soul; still she doubted, because of the unorthodoxy of it, and the remembrance of man and man alone being made in God's own image.

Still, through having no friend in whom to confide her new hope and happiness, the parrot became doubly dear to her. Curiously enough, in the succeeding weeks he was not so boisterous, he did not swear so much, but would sit watching his mistress as she sat dreaming, and now and then he said something which seemed inconceivable to her simple mind, unless he had a full understanding of the situation.

The minister came oftener and oftener; he stayed longer. He came home on Sunday nights with her after meeting. He kissed her at the door. He always held her little hand, which yielded to his with an indescribably gentle and innocent maidenliness, while he talked about the mission work in foreign lands, and always his lightest speech was set to that love-melody.

Martha began to expect to marry him. She overlooked her supply of linen. Visions of a new silk for a wedding-dress, brown instead of black, flashed before her eyes. She talked more than usual to the parrot in those

days, using the words and tone which she
might have used towards the minister, had
not the restraints of her New England
birth and training enclosed her like the wires
of a cage, and the parrot eyed her with wise
attentiveness which grew upon him, only now
and then uttering one of his favorite oaths.

Then suddenly the disillusion of the poor
soul as to her first gospel of love came. She
went to the sewing - circle one Wednesday
in early spring, after the minister had been
to see her for nearly a year, and she wore
her best black silk, thinking he would be
there, and she had crimped her hair and
looked as radiant as a girl when she entered
the low vestry filled with the discordant gab-
ble of sewing-women.

Then she heard the news. It was told
her with some protest and friendly prepara-
tion, for everybody had thought that the
match between herself and the minister was
as good as made. There was a whispered
discussion among groups of women, with
sly eyes upon her face; then one, who was
a leader among them, a woman of affectionate
glibness, approached her, after Martha had
heard a feminine voice lingering in the out-
skirts of a sudden hush say:

"She overlooked her supply of linen"

"And she's got on her best silk, too, poor thing."

Martha now looked up, and her radiant face paled slowly as the woman began to talk to her. The news seemed to smite her like some hammer of fate, her brain reeled, and her ears rang with it.

The minister was engaged, and had, in fact, gone to be married. He would bring his bride home the next week; another minister was to occupy his pulpit the next Sunday. He was to marry a woman to whom he had been attached for years, but the marriage had been delayed.

Martha listened, then suddenly the color flashed back into her white cheeks—she had stanch blood in her.

"Well, I am glad to hear it," she said, and lied with no compunction for the first time in her life, and never repented it. "I have always thought it was much better for a minister to be married," she said. "I have always thought that his usefulness would be much enhanced. Father used to say so." Then she took out her needle and thread and went to work with the others.

The women eyed her furtively, but she made no sign of noticing it. When one said to her that she had kind of thought that maybe the minister was shining up to her, she only laughed, and said gently that they were very good friends, but there had never been a word of anything else between them.

She overheard one woman whisper to another that, "if Martha was cut up, she would deceive the very elect," and the other reply, "that maybe he had told Martha all about the woman he was going to marry."

Martha stayed as usual to the supper and the entertainment. A young couple sat on a settee in front of her while some singing was going on, and at a tender passage she saw the boy furtively press the girl's hand, and she set her lips hard.

But at last she was free to go home, and when she had unlocked the door and entered her lonely house, down upon the floor in her sitting-room she flung herself, with all the floodgates of her New England nature open at last. She wept and wailed her grief and anger aloud like a Southern woman.

Then in the midst of it all came a wild wailing cry from the parrot, a cry of uncanny sympathy and pain and tenderness outside the pale of humanity.

"A gleam of affectionate oldness"

"Why, Martha! why, Martha! what's the matter?"

Then the woman rose and went to the cage, her delicate face and lips so swollen with grief that she was appalling; she had even trailed her best black silk in the mud on her way home. She was past the bounds of decency in her frenzy of misery. She opened the cage door, and the parrot flew out and to her slender shoulder, and she sobbed out her grief to him amid his protesting cries.

"Poor Martha, why, poor Martha," he said, and she felt almost certain that he had a soul, and she no longer felt so shocked by her leaning towards that belief, but was comforted.

But all of a sudden the parrot on her shoulder gave a tweak at her hair, and shrieked out:

"That was a damned cracker, Martha," and her belief wavered.

She put him back in his cage and locked up her house for the night, and put out her lamp and went to bed, but she could not go to sleep, for the loss of her old dream of love gave the whole world and all life such a hollowness and emptiness that it was like thunder in her ears, and forced its waking realization upon her.

All during the next week, if it had not been for the parrot, she felt that she would have gone mad. She went out in her small daily tracks to the village store, and the prayer-meetings, and on Sunday to church, her agony of concern being that no one should know that she was fretting over the minister's desertion of her.

She talked about the engagement and marriage with her gentle stateliness of manner, which never failed her, but when she got home to her parrot, and the healing solitariness of her own house, she felt like one who had a cooling lotion applied to a burn.

And she wondered more and more if the parrot had not verily a soul, and could not approach her with a sympathy which was better than any human sympathy, since it was so beyond all human laws, but she was not fully convinced of it until the minister brought his new wife to call upon her a few weeks after his marriage.

She had wondered vaguely if he would do it, if he could do it, but he came in with all his dashing grace of manner, and his bride was smiling at his side, in her wedding silks,

and Martha greeted them with no disturbance of her New England calm and stiffness, but inwardly her very soul stormed and protested; and as they were sitting in the parlor there came of a sudden from the next room, where he had been at large, the parrot, like a very whirlwind of feathered rage, and, with a wild shriek, he dashed upon the bridal bonnet, plucking furiously at roses and plumes.

Then there was a frightened and flurried exit, with confusion and apologies, and screams of baffled wrath, and rueful smoothing of torn finery.

And after the minister and his bride had gone, Martha looked at her parrot, and his golden eyes met hers, and she recognized in the fierce bird a comradeship and an equality, for he had given vent to an emotion of her own nature, and she knew forevermore that the parrot had a soul.

THE DOCTOR'S HORSE

THE DOCTOR'S HORSE

THE horse was a colt when he was purchased with the money paid by the heirs of one of the doctor's patients, and those were his days of fire. At first it was opined that the horse would never do for the doctor: he was too nervous, and his nerves beyond the reach of the doctor's drugs. He shied at every wayside bush and stone; he ran away several times; he was loath to stand, and many a time the doctor in those days was forced to rush from the bedsides of patients to seize his refractory horse by the bridle and soothe and compel him to quiet. The horse in that untamed youth of his was like a furnace of fierce animal fire; when he was given rein on a frosty morning the pound of his iron-bound hoofs on the rigid roads cleared them of the slow-plodding country teams. A current as of the very freedom and invincibility of life seemed to pass through the taut reins to the doctor's hands. But the doctor was the master of his horse, as of all other things with which he came in contact. He was a firm and hard man in the pursuance of his duty, never yielding to it with love, but unswervingly stanch. He was never cruel to his horse; he seldom whipped him, but he never petted him; he simply mastered him, and after a while the fiery animal began to go the doctor's gait, and not his own.

When the doctor was sent for in a hurry, to an emergency case, the horse stretched his legs at a gallop, no matter how little inclined he felt for it, perhaps on a burning day of summer. When there was no haste, and the doctor disposed to take his time, the horse went at a gentle amble, even though the frosts of a winter morning were firing his blood and every one of his iron nerves and muscles was strained with that awful strain of repressed motion. Even on those mornings the horse would stand at the door of the patient who was ill with old-fashioned consumption or chronic liver disease, his four legs planted widely, his head and neck describing a long downward curve, so expressive of submission and dejection

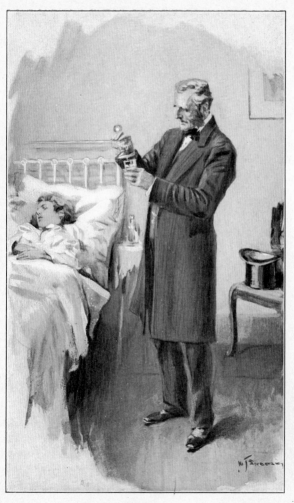

"*He was a firm and hard man in the pursuance of his duty*"

that it might have served as a hieroglyphic
for them, and no more thought of letting
those bounding impulses of his have their
way than if the doctor's will had verily bound
his every foot to the ground with unbreak-
able chains of servitude. He had become
the doctor's horse. He was the will of the
doctor, embodied in a perfect compliance
of action and motion. People remarked
how the horse had sobered down, what a
splendid animal. he was for the doctor, and
they had thought that he would never be able
to keep him and employ him in his profession.

Now and then the horse used to look
around at the empty buggy as he stood at
the gate of a patient's house, to see if the
doctor were there, but the will which held
the reins, being still evident to his consciousness, even when its owner was absent, kept
him in his place. He would have no thought
of taking advantage of his freedom; he would
turn his head and droop it in that curve of
utter submission, shift his weight slightly
to another foot, make a sound which was
like a human sigh of patience, and wait again.
When the doctor, carrying his little medicine-
chest, came forth, he would sometimes look
at him, sometimes not; but he would set

every muscle into an attitude of readiness for progress at the feel of the taut lines and the sound of the masterly human voice behind him.

Then he would proceed to the house of the next patient, and the story would be repeated. The horse seemed to live his life in a perfect monotony of identical chapters. His waiting was scarcely cheered or stimulated by the vision and anticipation of his stall and his supper, so unvarying was it. The same stall, the same measure of oats, the same allotment of hay. He was never put out to pasture, for the doctor was a poor man, and unable to buy another horse and to spare him. All the variation which came to his experience was the uncertainty as to the night calls. Sometimes he would feel a slight revival of spirit and rebellion when led forth on a bitter winter night from his stolidity of repose, broken only by the shifting of his weight for bodily comfort, never by any perturbation of his inner life. The horse had no disturbing memories, and no anticipations, but he was still somewhat sensitive to surprises. When the flare of the lantern came athwart his stall, and he felt the doctor's hand at his halter in the deep silence of a

midnight, he would sometimes feel himself
as a separate consciousness from the doctor,
and experience the individualizing of contrary desires.

Now and then he pulled back, planting
his four feet firmly, but he always yielded
in a second before the masterly will of the
man. Sometimes he started with a vicious
emphasis, but it was never more than mo-
mentary. In the end he fell back into his
state of utter submission. The horse was
not unhappy. He was well cared for. His
work, though considerable, was not beyond
his strength. He had lost something, undoubtedly, in this complete surrender of his
own will, but a loss of which one is unconscious tends only to the degradation of an
animal, not to his misery.

The doctor often remarked with pride that
his horse was a well-broken animal, somewhat stupid, but faithful. All the timid
women folk in the village looked upon him
with favor; the doctor's wife, who was nervous, loved to drive with her husband behind
this docile horse, and was not afraid even to
sit, while the doctor was visiting his patients,
with the reins over the animal's back. The
horse had become to her a piece of mechan-

ism absolutely under the control of her husband, and he was, in truth, little more. Still, a furnace is a furnace, even when the fire runs low, and there is always the possibility of a blaze.

The doctor had owned the horse several years, though he was still young, when a young woman came to live in the family. She was the doctor's niece, a fragile thing, so exposed as to her net-work of supersensitive nerves to all the winds of life that she was always in a quiver of reciprocation or repulsion. She feared everything unknown, and all strength. She was innately suspicious of the latter. She knew its power to work her harm, and believed in its desire to do so. Especially was she afraid of that rampant and uncertain strength of a horse. Never did she ride behind one but she watched his every motion; she herself shied in spirit at every wayside stone. She watched for him to do his worst. She had no faith when she was told by her uncle that this horse was so steady that she herself could drive him. She had been told that so many times, and her confidence had been betrayed. But the doctor, since she was like a pale weed grown in the shade, with no stimulus of life

except that given at its birth, prescribed fresh
air and, to her consternation, daily drives
with him. Day after day she went. She
dared not refuse, for she was as compliant in
her way to a stronger will as the horse. But
she went in an agony of terror, of which the
doctor had no conception. She sat in the
buggy all alone while the doctor visited his
patients, and she watched every motion of
the horse. If he turned to look at her, her
heart stood still.

And at last it came to pass that the horse
began in a curious fashion to regain something of his lost spirit, and met her fear of
him, and became that which she dreaded.
One day as he stood before a gate in late autumn, with a burning gold of maple branches
over his head and the wine of the frost in his
nostrils, and this timorous thing seated behind
him, anticipating that which he could but had
forgotten that he could do, the knowledge
and the memory of it awoke in him. There
was a stiff northwester blowing. The girl
was huddled in shawls and robes; her little,
pale face looked forth from the midst with
wide eyes, with a prospectus of infinite dan-
ger from all life in them; her little, thin hands
clutched the reins with that consciousness of

helplessness and conviction of the horse's power of mischief which is sometimes like an electric current firing the blood of a beast.

Suddenly a piece of paper blew under the horse's nose. He had been unmoved by fire-crackers before, but to-day, with that current of terror behind him firing his blood, that paper put him in a sudden fury of panic, of self-assertion, of rage, of all three combined. He snorted; the girl screamed wildly. He started; the girl gave the reins a frantic pull. He stopped. Then the paper blew under his nose again, and he started again. The girl fairly gasped with terror; she pulled the reins, and the terror in her hands was like a whip of stimulus to the evil freedom in the horse. She screamed again, and the sound of that scream was the climax. The horse knew all at once what he was— not the doctor, but a horse, with a great power of blood and muscle which made him not only his own master, but the master of all weaker things. He gave a great plunge that was rapture, the assertion of freedom— freedom itself — and was off. The faint screams of the frightened creature behind him stimulated him to madder progress.

" He thundered along the road "

At last he knew, by her terrified recognition of it, his own sovereignty of liberty.

He thundered along the road; he had no more thought of his pitiful encumbrance of servitude, the buggy, than a free soul of its mortal coil. The country road was cleared before him; plodding teams were pulled frantically to the side; women scuttled into door-yards; pale faces peered after him from windows. Now and then an adventurous man rushed into his path with wild halloos and a mad swinging of arms, then fled precipitately before his resistless might of advance. At first the horse had heard the doctor's shouts behind him, and had laughed within himself, then he left them far behind. He leaped, he plunged, his iron-shod heels touched the dashboard of the buggy. He heard splintering wood. He gave another lunging plunge, then he swerved and leaped a wall. Finally he had cleared himself of everything except a remnant of his harness. The buggy was a wreck, strewn piecemeal over a meadow. The girl was lying unhurt, but as still as if she were dead; but the horse which her fear had fired to new life was away in a mad gallop over the autumn fields, and his youth had returned. He was again him-

self—what he had been when he first awoke
to a consciousness of existence and the joy
of bounding motion in his mighty nerves
and muscles.   He was no longer the doctor's horse, but his own.

The doctor had to sell him.   After that
his reputation was gone, and, indeed, he was
never safe.   He ran away with the doctor.
He would not stand a moment unless tied, and
then pawed and pulled madly at the halter,
and rent the air with impatient whinnies.
So the doctor sold him, and made a good
bargain.   The horse was formed for speed,
and his lapse from virtue had increased his
financial value.   The man who bought him
had a good eye for horse-flesh, and had no
wish to stand at doors on his road to success,
but to take a bee-line for the winning-post.
The horse was well cared for, but for the first
time he felt the lash and heard curses; however, they only served to stimulate to a fiercer
glow the fire which had awakened within him.
He was never his new master's horse as he
had been the doctor's.   He gained the reputation of speed, but also of vicious nervous-
ness.   He was put on the race-course.   He
made a record at the county fair.   Once he
killed his jockey.   He used to speed along

the road drawing a man crouched in a tilting gig. Few other horses could pass him. Then he began to grow old.

At last, when the horse was old, he came into his first master's hands again. The doctor had grown old, older than the horse, and he did not know him at first, though he did say to his old wife that he looked something like that horse which he had owned which ran away and nearly killed his niece. After he said that, nothing could induce the doctor's wife to ride behind him; but the doctor, even in his feeble old age, had no fear, and the sidelong fire in the old horse's eye, and the proud cant of his neck, and his haughty resentment at unfamiliar sights on the road pleased him. He felt a confidence in his ability to tame this untamed thing, and the old man seemed to grow younger after he had bought the horse. He had given up his practice after a severe illness, and a young man had taken it, but he began to have dreams of work again. He never knew that he had bought his own old horse until after he had owned him some weeks. He was driving him along the country road one day in October when the oaks were a ruddy blaze, and the sumacs like torches along the walls, and the air like wine with the smell of grapes and apples. Then suddenly, while the doctor was sitting in the buggy with loose reins, speeding along the familiar road, the horse stopped; and he stopped before the house where had used to dwell the man afflicted with old-fashioned consumption, and the window which had once framed his haggard, coughing visage reflected the western sunlight like a blank page of gold. There the horse stood, his head and long neck bent in the old curve. He was ready to wait until the consumptive arose from his grave in the churchyard, if so ordered. The doctor stared at him. Then he got out and went to the animal's head, and man and horse recognized each other. The light of youth was again in the man's eyes as he looked at his own spiritual handiwork. He was once more the master, in the presence of that which he had mastered. But the horse was expressed in body and spirit only by the lines of utter yielding and patience and submission. He was again the doctor's horse.

BOUNCING BET

BOUNCING BET

IN July Bouncing Bet came again, appearing silently, with imperceptible gradations of progress, as was her wont. There were first an upflinging and outreaching as of tender naked fingers and arms; then came the unfolding of her stout, oval-lanceolate leaves; then the swelling of her buds; then that morning when the sun was hot and the wind blew in frequent soft gusts from the south she was present for the first time that year in her old place. She was almost identical with herself of the year before; there were no changes in her except those inevitable ones which pertain to the sequence of existence. She might be a little stockier, her roots might have thickened, but there were those same corymbs of loosely flapping, rose-colored flowers crowning her stout growth, exhaling the same odor, which was merely the breath of fresh life, not a compelling fragrance, as was the case with her cousins of the same race. She was far-removed kin to the garden pinks, exiled, none knew in what prehistoric age of flowers, from close relationship with them to the dusty, pilgrim ranks of the world, yet holding to life with undaunted zeal, and maintaining her own creed of bloom in spite of scorn and slights.

It was not so long since that she had been held in some honor; she had been planted and watered and tended; she had bloomed a welcome guest in a colonial garden. She was now like a dainty rag and shred of past fashion, left fluttering by the wayside from the passing of some former pageantry, but she knew no difference between her former estate and her last, being only a flower. Since her first setting in motion in her little cycle, her pendulum-swing between life and death, she had simply obeyed her law of creation. She was, indeed, obedience itself manifested in a clump of oval-lanceolate leaves of dusty green, and a meek, crowned head of delicate rose-colored flowers.

Behind Bouncing Bet was the remnant of the old garden where she had first seen life. Old Parson Lyman had planted the seeds, which he had brought over from England, in a border of his garden. The parson had been a gentle soul, fond of gentle things, like flowers and singing-birds and murmuring brooks and green grass. He had preached fire and brimstone with qualms of unbelief which he strove hard to swallow, and he died repenting with his last breath, and humbly confessing his inability to doubt the loving kindness and mercy of the Lord. Often in the parson's day the flower used to be overshadowed by a slender height of benignity, and regarded with affection by eyes which had not dwelt long upon things more material than flowers in the world. However, that made no difference to the flower, which was simply a thing set in motion by the old man's will, but immovable as to its principle of existence by any sentiment of his. The flower put to bloom by the man was as free as the man put to bloom by God.

This old parson had been a rich man, and his house had been accounted a mansion. After his death his married son came there to live. He had four daughters and two sons, one of whom afterwards died in the French and Indian War. Then came a time when, had the flower been alive in the fullest sense, she would have seen to remember. The garden was adorned by fairer things than flowers —by damsels in hooped petticoats of silks more gorgeous than the roses; there was an arbor where lovers sat, and the air was full of the mystery of love. Then all that passed, and more of the same, and the past lay more and more thickly buried under the past, and finally, when Bouncing Bet returned in this hot July, everything was so changed as almost to have passed that limit of change where identity ceases.

The road had widened, the old garden had retreated. Bouncing Bet was far beyond the precincts in the common highway along with the common weeds, herself a weed, if she were ranked with her intimates. The stately old house leaned heavily towards its fall, its gambrel roof sagged, there were patches of moss and mould in the hollows, its walls were flapping with gray shingles, and in it lived alone the last survivor of the line of the old parson who planted the flower. The last survivor was a woman, of course. It is generally the woman who survives, either from her pliability of strength, which no storm nor stress can affect, or from the fact that she holds to existence with less te-

"The last survivor was a woman"

nacity of grasp, and so does not waste her life with her effort to save it.

Be that as it may, she lived alone there, her husband and children being so long dead that she thought of them with the utter peace of acquiescence. She had, indeed, acquiesced, with no questioning, in most of the decrees of fate. She had a placid temperament, and was disposed to get her honey from small things in lieu of great ones. People said that she had not felt her trials as most would have done, and, in proof of it, pointed to her face, young beyond her years, with a blowsy, yet delicate, bloom of round cheeks, a calm clearness of blue eyes, and smooth crinkles of yellow hair. "Any woman that can go through what Ann Lyman has gone through and not have a gray hair hasn't got feelings," said they, especially Mrs. John Evarts, who lived in her daughter's new house across the street. Mrs. John Evarts, who kept house in the north side, used to sit in her bay-window and watch proceedings over the way. She was the one who instigated the plan to take Ann from her old home and have her board with Mrs. Jackson Smith, with whom the town occasionally boarded people whose former estate and some remnant of present means seemed to prohibit from the town farm. Mrs. Jackson Smith was, moreover, a distant relative of the Lymans, and that made it seem a milder measure.

"It won't seem anything but going to live with her cousin," said Mrs. John Evarts. She furthermore said that she had lain awake nights worrying over it. She knew Ann Lyman would set herself afire, she would starve to death, she would bring an epidemic of typhoid into the neighborhood, living the way she did.

Poor Ann Lyman's easy acquiescence in circumstances extended to conditions of natural dirt and disorder. It is possible that it might have extended as well to original sin had her lines been cast in different places. Her neighbors, the rigorously tidy village women, said that Ann Lyman couldn't see dirt; possibly she might not have seen sin had it come in her way; but it never had. That had not been so inevitable. The dust of life had not come in her windows to settle on her soul, but the dust of the country roads had entered and settled on her furniture, and she let it remain.

"I don't believe you ever dust, Ann Lyman," Mrs. Evarts said one day.

Ann only laughed.

"Do you?" insisted the other woman, scowling above her forced smile.

"No," said Ann.

Ann might have argued, with justice, that she had not much worth dusting. Piece by piece the stately old furniture of the mansion-house had been disposed of to the dealers. There was now little left; the paint was worn from the fine panel-work, and rags of carpets clung to the nails on the edges of the slanting floors, but Ann could accomplish a great multiple of disorder with few factors. The interior of the old house resembled nothing so much as the interior of a wrecked ship. Its broken furnishings were all set askance at one another, every shred of former splendor was in full and defiant evidence, and, in addition, there was a general effect of all the lines of construction being awry and off their true levels. There was not a horizontal line in the whole house; there were only the reckless slants of waste and destruction by that fiercest storm of the world, the storm of time. But all this did not trouble Ann in the least. When a rocker of her old chair, in which she had sat by her favorite window for more than forty years, gave out, she put a stick of wood in its place, and sat still, and concluded that she fancied that better than rocking. When the glass was broken out of her favorite window, she moved over to another, and thought the new outlook pleasanter. Every new groove of life had fitted this easily sliding, jelly-like old woman; she took her shape from circumstances; nothing rubbed her to her discomfort; she was the happiest woman in the village. But her time came.

The afternoon the selectmen, headed by Jonathan Lyman, the far-away kinsman of the old Lyman family to which she and the old house belonged, came to interview her about the proposed change in her way of living, there was a transformation. This smoothly-oscillating-at-every-touch creature became of a sudden vibrant with pure individuality. Her flaccid muscles seemed to harden, the faint bloom on her cheeks blazed, her loosely smiling mouth was rigid, her mild eyes pointed as with the glitter of steel. All human beings, however unassertive they may be, have some footholds of self, impregnable against assault. Ann's had been touched, and she stood firm with a great shock of revolt. She stood up, clinched and stiffened; her voice rang out with such

"*She used to sit in the bay-window*"

an echo that the selectmen turned simultaneously and stared over their shoulders.

There were three of the selectmen; two
were elderly, the third was young Lyman.
He had been pushed forward to do the speaking to Ann. He had opened glibly enough.
He was confident by nature, and of an imperious turn. Then, too, his sweetheart
was Mrs. John Evarts's granddaughter,
and she had advised this measure. He
stated, pitilessly candid, and yet with no
thought that his candor was pitiless, being
one of those to whom the truth is its own
vindication, the facts of the case. He pointed out to this lone woman her poverty, her
untidiness, her lack of thrift, her indolence;
he descanted upon the injury to herself and
others; he descanted upon the superior advantages of the home which had been provided for her; he mentioned the fact that
the savings-bank held an overdue mortgage
on the property; he concluded by ordering
Ann to be in readiness to move the next day.

But even he, as well as his colleagues, was
aghast at the result. When they turned to
face Ann after that first incredulous glance
over shoulders for some other source of that
unexpected voice, each had the same help-

less gape of astonishment. They listened speechless, too amazed to shuffle in their chairs.

"This old house," said Ann, with a ringing eloquence of desperation—"this old house has belonged to my father's family for over a hundred years, and you talk about turning me out of it! Me! Me! Why don't you turn the chimney out? Why don't you pull down the door-post? I'm as much a part of it. Root up the box out in the yard; pull up that clump of pinies; tear up the lilac bushes; chop down the poplar-tree that my grandfather planted! Pull down, root up, but I tell you leave me be! I belong here! I am the live thing that keeps it together. What if I ain't neat? What's neatness to things that belong to life itself, I want to know? What if I ain't orderly? Ain't I alive? I tell you I'm the soul of this old place, and you want to turn a soul out of a body! I was born here, and my father before me, and my grandfather before him. I lived right along here when I was married; my children were born here, and they all died here. Talk about the savings-bank holding a mortgage! What's a mortgage? You can't mortgage things with any show of reason that are a part and parcel of a human being. Turn *me* out! Me! Me!"

Suddenly Ann sat down in her broken rocking-chair again, and a curious defiance of immovability seemed to settle over her. She actually looked as if it would need more than human strength to dislodge her. She in her rocking-chair seemed as rigidly impossible of movement as the pyramids.

The two elder selectmen looked at the young chairman. There was a flush on his cheeks. He arose.

"Well, Mrs. Lyman," said he, "I regret to see that you are in such a frame of mind, but my opinion remains the same, and so will that of all your friends. At two o'clock to-morrow I will be here with a carriage, and I must beg that you will be ready."

Ann made no reply, but she looked at him as if her soul was rooted fast in all the ages.

The three selectmen went out. One of them, quite an old man, was fairly pale. "She's going to take on terribly about going," he said to the chairman, who smiled scornfully. There was a cruel vein in him; his handsome face was quite unmoved.

The next afternoon he presented himself at the old house without his colleagues, who had excuses ready for their absence. He fastened the horse, hitched in a large covered wagon, to the old post at the gate; then he went up to the front door and raised the knocker. He waited, but no one came. He knocked again, with no better result. He looked at the windows, which were dusty blanks. He glanced across the way, and saw Mrs. John Evarts standing in her front door watching curiously. A girl's pretty, fair face looked over her shoulder, and he knew it for his sweetheart's, Flora Evarts. After he had knocked again in vain, she came running over, her grandmother following, and presently her aunt Hannah, who lived in the house, and had just returned from making calls, and wore her black silk, which rustled a good deal and tinkled with jet, and a bonnet nodding with grasses.

Thus reinforced, the selectman opened the front door and entered the house. A shadow moved across the old hall with the spiral stair in the midst, and they all started; but it was only due to a curtain in an open window swaying in the sudden draught from the door. They went through all the squalid rooms. The little party became gradually augmented until nearly all the neighbors

were there. Most of them were women.
They opened door after door; they eyed the
revelations of squalor with disgust and a
growing horror. "Something's happened
to her," one and another whispered. They
peered fearfully into close clothes-presses;
they searched the evil-smelling cellar glooms
and the long, dusty shadows under the garret eaves. All the party fell back with pale,
shocked faces, even the chairman of the selectmen, at the sight of an old gown hanging
from a high bedpost. But young Lyman's
terror was over in a moment; he was to the
front, and had gingerly dislodged the gar-
ment.

"To think of a Christian woman wearing
a dress like that!" said Mrs. John Evarts.
The old woman held her skirts wrapped
closely around her thin figure; she held her
nose averted, ready with a sniff of disgust.
The malice in her was only half intimidated
by the fear of what she might at any minute
see in these poor rooms. She had never loved
Ann Lyman, and the reason therefor dated
back to their girlhood. The flaws of her
neighbor had been her chief savor of life,
and she was tasting it now to the uttermost.

At last they had searched the old house

from garret to cellar, and Ann was not there. There could be no doubt of it. They all stood together in the north chamber and conferred as to the situation. The north chamber had been the guest-room of the old mansion, and was in some respects the best preserved. There was still a decent straw matting on the floor, and an ancient green-and-white paper on the walls, and the ceiling was not precarious. There lingered also the splendid carved bureau and the high-posted bedstead. Ann had refused to sell these, on account of associations, the violation of which even her placidity could not face. "My husband had his last sickness in this room," she told the dealer, "and it was fitted up for me with a new carpet when I was married. I'm going to let it be a while longer." It was in this room that the one attempt at housewifery was evident. The great feather-bed hung from the window to air, suspended on the stout blind-hooks.

"I didn't know she ever aired anything," remarked Mrs. John Evarts, in a harsh whisper.

Flora looked at her disapprovingly.

"You don't know but she's dead, grandmother," said she.

"I should be ashamed to be dead and leave a house looking like this," said her grandmother, stoutly.

"She's run away," suggested one of the neighbors.

"She's drowned herself in the well, mebbe," whispered another, trembling.

"She must have felt pretty desperate, poor thing!" said Mrs. John Evarts's daughter. There were glass dew-drops on the nodding grasses on her bonnet, and they tinkled as did the jet beads on her bodice; the silken breadths of her dress rustled, and her best shoes creaked when she eased her weight. She was a stout woman; her cheeks were blazing, and her mouth drooped piteously at the corners. "I wish you hadn't said anything about her to the selectmen," she said to her mother.

"Look at this house," retorted Mrs. John Evarts.

"Well, you might have let her be as long as she lived," said her daughter. "She didn't hurt anybody but herself with the dirt."

"She didn't, hey?" retorted the old woman. She leaned over her daughter, and whispered fiercely some further disclosures as to the missing woman's untidiness and actual indecency of squalor; but her daughter only shook her tinkling head; "I'm dreadful sorry you did anything about it," she repeated.

Suddenly, as they all stood there conferring as to what was best to be done next, the girl, Flora Evarts, in her pretty pink muslin dress, with a pink rose tucked in her belt, gave a great start. They all turned and looked at her.

"What on earth is the matter, Flora?" cried her grandmother, sharply.

"Nothing," replied the girl, quickly; but her pretty face was very pale.

The young selectman stepped close to her and looked at her anxiously, but she turned her back on him sharply.

"What ails you all?" she cried, pettishly. "If there isn't enough to make anybody jump! Why don't you go and have the well dragged and send out some parties to search, and not stand here talking any longer?"

"What made you jump so, Flora?" persisted the selectman.

"Nothing, I tell you," said the girl, sharply. Then she turned with sudden passion. "For

Heaven's sake," she demanded, "why don't you do something? That poor soul will die if somebody doesn't do something." She caught her breath in a sob, and again the selectman looked at her anxiously and wonderingly. He had never seen her like that. She was a girl of remarkable poise. But her energy moved them all. They dispersed, to drag the well and a near-by pond, and to organize searching-parties. Not one of the neighbors had seen her pass. It was as if the old woman had vanished.

At last the north chamber was quite deserted. The last woman had been gone a minute or so, when Flora Evarts came speeding back like a deer. She rushed to the window where the feather-bed hung. She caught hold of it; she leaned over it.

"Are you there?" she whispered. "Answer quick. Don't be afraid. Are you there?"

There was a slight convulsive motion of the feather-bed, but no other response.

"Don't be afraid. They sha'n't take you away if you don't want to go," repeated the girl. "Are you there? Are you most dead? I must help you out! Answer me. I'm Flora Evarts! I'll take care of you! Are you there?"

Then there came a stifled groan, then a gasping sob from the feather-bed. Then the girl, grasping the edge of the bed with two nervous little hands, began to tug frantically. She heard a slight sound of rending cloth. The bed wriggled convulsively. Flora cast a glance of horror at the ground below. It was not far into the growth of sweetbrier and caraway bushes beneath the window in the back yard, but it was too far to fall.

"Reach out your arms if you can," she cried; and up came, with a desperate effort, two skinny, piteous old arms, and the girl clutched them.

"Oh, you poor soul!" she half sobbed. "Don't be afraid; don't be afraid."

"You let go if I've got to be carried away," said a muffled voice. She could see the struggling shape of the old woman's head in the feather-bed. The tick tore a little more at the hooks. Flora held to the lean old hands desperately. She braced her feet and pulled. Somehow she managed it. Ann got her feet on the edge of the window below, and helped herself a little. Finally she fell into the north chamber, and she and the girl sank on the floor together. Flora struggled to her feet

and helped the old woman out of the feather-
bed. She was grotesquely tragic, her cheeks
shining with heat, her eyes red-rimmed like
an owl's; she was bristling with feathers.
But she held herself with a dignity of misery which forbade mirth.

"I knew they would find me anywhere
else," said she. "I didn't care if I did fall
and break my neck. I heard it tear while
you all stood here. You heard it, didn't you,
Flora?"

Flora nodded. She kept her mouth firmly set, but the tears were streaming over her
cheeks.

"You won't let them take me away, will
you, Flora?"

"No, I won't," declared Flora, in a firm
voice. She heard just then a noise below,
and she flung open the north chamber door
and called. Her lover, the selectman, answered her.

"Come here," said Flora.

"I'm after a rope—I can't stop," he returned.

"You don't need any rope. She's here,"
said Flora.

The young man came rushing up-stairs,
but Flora stood in the north chamber door.

"You can't come in; you can't touch her," she declared.

"Flora!"

"You sha'n't take away this woman from this house as long as she lives!"

"Flora!"

"You shall not, I say."

"But—"

"If you do, I will never marry you as long as I live," said Flora.

With that she flung up her hands, still cramped with the effort of holding to those other helpless ones of the poor old woman, and the young man caught her in his arms.

The old woman slipped past them and went down-stairs to her place by the window. She leaned her head back in her rickety chair, and smiled with perfect contentment. She did not trouble herself to pick off any of the feathers still clinging to her garments. She was beyond such matters, as much beyond as any flower of the field at the mercy of the wings of winds and settling foreign things.

After a while her kind neighbors came and assured her that she should remain in her old home as long as she lived. Mrs. John Evarts tidied up the kitchen and made her a cup of tea. Flora brought in some floating-island, and another woman some custard-pie. When the last one went away her larder was quite full.

At sunset Ann Lyman crept out to her front door-step and sat there in the full of the passing radiance. Beyond the gate bloomed the clump of Bouncing Bet. Mrs. John Evarts looked across from her window and saw them both—the old woman and the flower, both with a strange unkemptness of late bloom, both fulfilling to the utmost their one law of obedience to their first conditions of life. And she also saw, without comprehension, two parallels, separated perhaps by the width of the eternity of the spirit, yet as perfect and undeviating as any on the terrestrial globe.

PRINCE'S-FEATHER

PRINCE'S-FEATHER

GAYLY above the tangled spangle of the old-fashioned garden waved the prince's-feather. It waved with a curious lack of yielding and pliability to the soft insinuations of the breeze, and seemed to remain long in its rigid incline, almost as if the flower had been carven in rosy stone blown before some wind of the imagination. The prince's-feather belonged to the order of amaranthine flowers which resist complete decay, being armed against it like porcupines with stiff panoplies of spikes.

One coming down the street, peering over the garden-hedge of the Holding place, saw always first the prince's-feather. There were fairer and sweeter flowers, but that came first in evidence, thrusting itself like a trumpet call of color above the mignonette, the sweet alyssum, the pinks, and the rest. Even the tall hollyhocks, being retired against the house wall, were eclipsed. The prince's-feather seemed to overcap and lead the floral riot of midsummer with a harmless and worthless, but unrivalled show and daring.

The garden was in a hollow at the right of the Holding house, which was very old, but had lately been improved and rejuvenated until it seemed disrespectful, to either its age or its youth, to remember its old corner-stones and sills, the drunken leanings and waverings of its doors and windows, the undulations of its floors, and the settling and shortening of its central chimney like some aged man whose stature has decreased by years. Eugene Holding had suddenly become rich, and had restored the old place, throwing out, like ostentatious excrescences of a new growth, porticos, bay-windows, and even a tower crowned with a cupola on the corner towards the village square.

Eugene was very young when he came home from the city where he had been employed, working his way up—for the fortunes of the family were at the lowest ebb—in a great machine factory owned by a distant kinsman of his mother. Immediately after he had arrived, the news spread that he had come into such a fortune that the working up was unnecessary, since the height was gained.

One evening in May, at sundown, young Eugene came riding into town on the driver's seat of the stage-coach which plied between the village and the nearest railroad centre. Instead of the little hair-cloth trunk, like some small animal of an extinct species, with which he had gone away, two modern affairs of smooth leather were strapped on behind. As for Eugene himself, he was radiant, fairly resplendent. He sat beside the driver, and, although the other man was over the average size, he seemed to be head and shoulders above him. He looked abroad with a gay confidence in admiration which compelled it. His handsome face was delicately pink and white, with a daintily curving golden mustache. His close crop of curly golden hair was exposed, for he was constantly waving his hat to people on the road. They returned his salutations with the surly abashedness of the rustic, then stood back and stared and stared again. "Who was that?" one said to another. "It wasn't Eugene Holding. Why, he's workin' in Philadelphia. He can't be home this time of year, and all dressed up that way." The hue of Eugene's coat had struck awe and disapproval to the hearts of the men. There was no other coat of that color in the village.

Before sundown the next day Eugene's mother had told the news to Mrs. William Holmes and to Mrs. Catherine Woods, and they did the rest. The whole village knew, as by a flash of simultaneous intelligence, that Eugene Holding had made money and had come home rich. "He will not need to do anything more as long as he lives," said Eugene's mother. She had a face harsh in color and outline, yet, curiously enough, exceedingly gentle in expression; she was slender and tall, with a settled stoop which was not ungraceful, being lateral. One meeting Mrs. Holding thought involuntarily of a strong starboard wind, and realized dimly an incongruity between her attitude of body and her motionless skirts. Mrs. Holding was unusually precise as to her choice of language, being punctilious as to her will nots and shall nots, and disdaining contractions. People in consequence called her affected. They were inwardly resentful and skeptical when they saw her triumph over her son. "How did he make his money?" asked Mrs. William Holmes, with a cold stare, though she widened her mouth in a smile of congratulation.

"My son has been exceedingly fortunate in a business venture, and he will not need to lift his finger again unless he wants to," said Mrs. Holding, adjusting a lacy crocheted hood which she wore over her head.

"How did you say he made it?" repeated the other woman.

"By a fortunate business measure," replied Mrs. Holding.

"Seems to me Eugene is pretty young to make such fortunate business ventures," said Mrs. Holmes. "How did you say he made his money?"

"By a fortunate business venture," said Mrs. Holding.

That was all she ever would say, and Eugene, in spite of his aggressiveness of frankness, was no more communicative as to the source of his wealth, about which there seemed to be no doubt. He commenced immediately to improve his house, and he purchased a fine horse and carriage. It was an imposing spectacle when Eugene drove forth in the cool of a summer evening, at first with his mother resplendent in a new silk, a beflowered bonnet, and a jetted mantle, by his side, and, later on, Camilla Rose.

Camilla Rose's father had been the richest man in the village; she had money in her own right, and had "enjoyed advantages," as the neighbors put it. "Good reason why Camilla Rose can look so nice and appear so pretty," said they. "She ought to; she's been to boarding-school, and she's travelled in Europe." They were enviously acquiescent when she and Eugene began to be seen in each other's company. "Birds of a feather flock together," said they. "Of course, now Eugene has got money, Camilla will think he's beautiful. The Roses always had an eye for money. Besides, his family counts for something. The Holdings and the Roses always held their heads above common folks." This Camilla Rose was a tall, brown-eyed girl, with a pouting redness of lips, and a reluctant smile, which gathered charm from its reluctance. Whoever made Camilla smile at him was conscious of a distinct victory. Camilla smiled upon Eugene rarely, yet often enough to keep alive in him a supporting sense of encouragement.

However, it would not have been easy for her to have discouraged Eugene Holding.

Anything like the joyful sanguinity of this young fellow was seldom seen. He seemed furnished by nature with some armor of the spirit which rendered him impervious to slight and repulse. His mother was proud of this peculiarity in her son. "If anybody has ever said no to Eugene, he has gone right ahead and acted as if he had said yes," said she. "Then there is another thing about Eugene—if ever he has been so situated that he could not have something that he set his heart upon, another would do just as well, and he never seemed to know that he had not got what he wanted. I remember once when he had been longing for a new jack-knife, somebody gave him a top instead, and he went right to spinning it, and never seemed to know he was not whittling. I never heard him mention the knife again. Eugene always gets ahead of his happenings, and he always will. Nothing that can ever happen on this earth is going to conquer him. He is bound to be in the lead of his fate." Mrs. Holding was something of a philosopher, and talked sometimes beyond her neighbors. That and her precise English caused them to regard her half with admiration, half with the defensive ridicule of inferiority. They

regarded Eugene in something of the same
fashion. "He ain't so smart, for all he
cuts such a dash," said they. "His mother
needn't think he is; he ain't." They looked
at him as he drove by, or walked with a gentle swagger, and a jaunty swing of a slender
cane, and frequent flourishes of his silk hat,
yet, after all, they felt a certain admiration
and liking for him. It was impossible not
to like Eugene Holding. His utter confidence of approval commanded it. One would
have been a churl not to smile back at this
forever-smiling young man, not to return
with some cordiality his imperious, but
wholly charming, even affectionate, saluta-
tion. "Eugene Holding acts as if he was
the lord of all creation," said they, yet with a
certain self-gratulation at having been so
genially accosted by one of such high pre-
tensions.

Eugene and Camilla were such a handsome couple that they were a delight to the
eye when they were seen driving together.
Eugene was taller than the girl; his golden
curly head gleamed beside her brown one.
Camilla's beautiful face was shaded by a
great cloud of brown curls, and a blue feather
floated from her Leghorn hat. She was as

"Eugene and Camilla were seen driving together"

pleasantly conscious of the people whom they met, and their admiration, as she was of the young man at her side.

Eugene thought Camilla perfection. He adored her beauty, yet the memory of it never dimmed for a moment the image of his own face in the mirror. He always saw her pretty gowns and hats, and the sight sent his consideration with the swift recoil of vanity to his own apparel.

Eugene hurried forward the improvements on his house; they were completed in July, and he and Camilla were to be married the first of August. The villagers passing the renovated house used to turn back and stare, and that made Eugene and his mother, sitting on their new porch, proudly conscious.

Eugene took an especial delight in the little cupola which crowned the tower. The cupola was purely ornamental, and the roof was painted a bright crimson color, not unlike that of the prince's-feather in the garden. Indeed, it might have been unconsciously suggested by it. Eugene used to stand out in the front yard and stare happily at this brilliant cupola.

"Your new cupola looks very gay," said Camilla's mother to Mrs. Holding one afternoon as the two ladies sat on the porch. She did not speak critically; that was not her way. She simply mentioned facts, and left her hearers to deduce disparagement or flattery as they chose. Mrs. Holding, like her son, generally deduced flattery. "Yes, it is a beautiful color," said she. "Eugene has always been so fond of bright colors."

As she spoke Eugene and Camilla came across the yard on their way from the garden, and Eugene had a sprig of prince's-feather waving against the lapel of his coat. He had also stuck a great spike of it like a plume in Camilla's curls.

As the two neared the porch Camilla reached up her hand and pulled out the prince's-feather and flung it away. "I never liked that flower," she remarked.

"It is the prettiest flower in the garden," declared Eugene, but he only laughed at her scorn of it, and flung an arm around the girl's waist, and they came thus towards the two mothers. There was a strong south wind blowing, and the two tall figures stiffened themselves against it. Camilla seemed in a whirlwind of white flounces and ribbons, out of which her beautiful face looked with unsmiling complacency, which was, in effect, a smile at herself. Eugene had just given her some diamond ear-drops, which glittered through her curls; she had everything which she wanted; a measureless satisfaction with herself, the whole world, and the Providence which had created her was over the girl, and no less over the young man. Both of them looked invincible by any fate. They had the mien of conquerors as they came across the yard, with the two elders watching them, the one with perfect accord, the other with pride and delight, yet with bewilderment. Camilla's mother was sometimes bewildered almost to the point of fear by her daughter. She herself had never been capable of such a haughty confidence in the good-will of Providence, but was rather prepared for a sanctified and gentle acquiescence towards hard usage on its part. Mrs. Holding realized dimly that Camilla had an almost contemptuous, and her lover a joyfully imperious, incredulity that the tree of life could grow anything but plums for them, and she herself was conscious of a guilty wonder if it would not be unworthy so to do, in the face of such superb confidence.

Mrs. Holding, while she had the greatest pride in Camilla, yet felt herself more in sympathy with her younger daughter Jane, although she had a peevish temper, and was semi-crippled. One of Jane's limbs was shorter than the other, and she limped about with a painful absurdity of gait, which tortured her soul even more than her body. Jane would never walk beside Camilla. She used to watch her sister set out to drive with her handsome lover, as some utterly irredeemable Cinderella might have done. It did not seem as if existence could ever hold glass slippers and a gold coach for her, least of all a prince; but such things are always unexpected, and her day came, though in what might have seemed a half-hearted and second-rate sort of fashion. The week before Eugene and Camilla were to be married, the young man came to visit his sweetheart one evening, and he was gayer and more unconcerned than ever. They went to drive, and it was like a triumphal progress. Eugene bowed to every one with that charming, almost royal, assurance of conferring a favor and a grace. Camilla sat beside him like a queen. It was not until they reached her gate on their return that he told her the news, laughing as he did so, as if it were the pleasantest thing in the world.

"The mine has gone to pieces," said he, easily.

"What mine?" asked Camilla, in bewilderment. "What do you mean?"

"The mine has gone to pieces, or, rather, there isn't any mine. There never was. Isn't it a joke, eh?"

"What mine?"

"The one I put the little money we had left in," said Eugene, smiling. "That was how I got my money, you know, or, rather, my prospects. I never got much money, but nobody ever had such prospects. Why, Camilla, we might have had the earth. Never was such a mine as they made that out to be."

Camilla had turned very pale. "What do you mean?" she said, slowly. "Haven't you got any money, Eugene?"

"Not a dollar," he returned, laughing; "had two big dividends, and paid for the cupola and things, and mother's clothes and mine, and your diamonds—that's all. Not a dollar left. I didn't tell you what my money was in, you know, because the prospects were so big. I wanted to surprise you. Never were such prospects. Camilla, you ought to have seen the diamond brooch I was looking at for you last week."

"Are you going to work in your old place again?" asked Camilla, in a queer voice.

"Oh no," Eugene replied, cheerfully. "I am going to stay on here, and raise early vegetables. I think I can make a good thing with early vegetables. I dare say you'll get that brooch before the year is out, after all, Camilla."

"You don't expect to marry me next week?" she said.

"Why—why not?" cried Eugene, not with dismay, but a merry, childlike incredulousness that she could mean what she said.

Camilla said no more. She motioned to get out of the carriage, and Eugene sprang out to assist her. He caught her in his arms and kissed her. "Good-night," he called after her as she went up the path. "I'll be around to-morrow night." Then he drove away, and his merry whistle floated back above the rattle of the wheels and the tap of the horse's hoofs.

The next evening, when Eugene came to take Camilla driving, she did not meet him at the door as usual, all ready in her pretty gown and hat.

He sat waiting, several people passed, and he saluted them in his ordinary manner, and they returned it and went on whispering. They had heard the news that he had lost his money—that he had never had any money. He had been more confidential over his loss than over his acquisition. He had told everybody at length all the details of the spurious mining venture, and had not a word of reproach for those who had deceived him. On the contrary, he seemed to feel nothing but gratitude.

"They told me there was a wonderful prospect ahead, and so there was," said he. Then he would add that if it had not been for that he might have worked in a factory all his days, and never been led to think of raising early vegetables, in which scheme he had even more confidence than he ever had in the mine. He had in his pockets some packages of seeds which he had purchased that afternoon, though he could not plant them until the next spring. He took them out and examined them delightedly as he waited. He had brought them to show to Camilla.

But Camilla did not appear. He was just about to get out and go to the door when it opened, and the younger sister Jane stood there. "Hello, Jane," Eugene called out.

"Tell Camilla to hurry. Dick doesn't like to stand. The flies plague him."

Jane did not answer, but came painfully limping out to the carriage. Then she spoke, looking at him with terror and distress, and something else, which was adoration, but he did not know it.

"Camilla isn't going to drive with you, Eugene," said she.

"Isn't going to drive with me? Why not? Why, what makes you look so pale, Jane? Are you sick?"

"No. Camilla isn't going to drive with you, Eugene."

"Is she sick?"

"No, she isn't sick. She isn't going to drive with you."

"Why not?" Eugene stared. Suddenly he fumbled in his pocket and pulled out a little pink note. "See here," he cried, "I had this letter from Camilla, but I didn't dream she meant it. She didn't mean it, did she?"

Jane's face quivered a little, though her eyes were hard. "Yes, she did," said she. "Camilla has always meant it, if she is my sister."

"She meant it?" repeated Eugene, incredulously. "Why, I never dreamed it. She says," he continued, eying the letter, "that she can't marry me on account of the change in my prospects. Why, my prospects haven't changed! She says she feels that she is not suited to be the wife of a poor man. Why, I am not a poor man, and my prospects haven't changed! Say, Jane, did she tell you about the early vegetables?"

Jane did not reply to that. She only repeated, in a sort of mechanical fashion, "Camilla isn't going to drive with you."

"Oh, nonsense!" cried Eugene; "of course she is. Go in and tell her, that's a good girl, Jane. Tell her I want to show her the seeds I've got. I guess she won't think my prospects have changed, then. Go in and tell her, Jane, do."

"I can't," said Jane, half angrily, half piteously. Her little face was a study of conflicting emotions.

"Well, then," said Eugene, good-humoredly, "I must go in and fetch her myself. Stand by the horse a minute, will you, Jane?"

Jane threw up her hand to stop him. "No," she cried out. "No, no! It's no use! Oh, it isn't any use, Eugene!"

Eugene stared at her. "Why isn't it any

use? Of course she 'll go. It'll be all right when I tell her."

"Camilla isn't at home," faltered Jane.

"Camilla isn't at home?"

"No, she has gone to Boston. She went over to Barnstable to get the noon train." With that Jane began crying.

Eugene was silent for a minute. His bright face had the obscured look of a flower when the shadow of a cloud passes over it, but it soon cleared. He looked at Camilla's sister, who stood before him, balancing herself painfully on her unequal limbs, trying to control her tears, and he laughed with his unconquerable gayety and good humor.

"Oh, well," said Eugene, "if Camilla has gone to Boston, she has lost a fine drive, and why don't you go instead, Jane?"

"Me?"

"Yes, why not? Run and put on your hat, for the horse doesn't like to stand. The flies plague him."

When people saw Eugene Holding driving with Jane Rose instead of her sister, they could not credit their own eyes. Indeed, several were always incredulous, and believed it to have been Camilla, and the plain girl attired in a hat and gown like her beautiful

sister's did bear at a distance a curious resemblance to her. It was the same resemblance which a misshapen flower bears to another of the same family. They skimmed
along the smooth country road.

Suddenly Eugene cast a startled look at
his companion. "Why, you look like Camilla, Jane!" he cried. "I declare you do.
Did any one ever tell you so?"

"No," gasped Jane.

"Well, you do," said Eugene, "and I declare, Jane, you look more like her than you
did when I spoke first. I want to show you
these seeds I have got. It's odd that Camilla
should have thought I have lost my prospects."

To this poor little Jane the prospect of a
crown and a throne would have been as nothing beside the fact of the prince. Eugene
married Jane the 1st of September. In
the mean time Camilla returned from Boston betrothed to another man. She had always more than one string to her bow. Eugene heard the news with a face which defied the scrutiny of even Jane's jealous eyes.
He did not shun Camilla at all; he even
jested about her engagement and his own.

"You would not have me, Camilla," he

said, "because you thought my prospects were changed. You were wrong as to that, for my prospects are not changed; they are better than ever. But that has nothing to do with it. We are both suited, after all. I hear you will have a fine husband, and as for me, I'm going to be in your family, just the same. I've got your sister, and she's a darling. I never dreamed what a darling she was, and I would never have known if it hadn't been for you. She is going to make me a wonderful wife, and she looks like you."

Camilla stared at him, but he smiled back at her. He was speaking from the depths of his impregnable and innocently unconscious egotism, which surpassed her own, and she felt herself overmatched.

Later on Eugene's wife became an invalid. Her peevishness increased, and even love and happiness could not transform her. Eugene would have led a sorry life with her had he known it, but he never did. He firmly believed that he had the loveliest and most amiable wife in the world. His vegetable scheme failed; then he tried bees, then small fruits. Everything failed except his hope and faith in himself and his future success. That never for a moment failed him. There

"The most amiable wife in the world"

was something splendid about the man. He
became, as it were, a very Napoleon of his
own fortunes. Nothing in the hand of fate
could daunt him. He was invulnerable to
circumstances, half laughed at, half admired by all who knew him. His mother
died, his means decreased, he often went
without the necessaries of life, his house,
which he had so improved, became a shabby
travesty on his former fortunes, he grew old,
but new mountain-tops of hope never failed
to enliven his failing eyes and encourage
his faltering feet.

The garden at the right of the Holding
house grew old, unplanted, and untended,
but the prince's-feather never failed to come
to the front, proudly waving in all its first
splendor above the disordered hosts of flowers and weeds. And always to the front in
the unfailing spring of all his winters of defeat pressed the man, raising aloft his shining
head, which never grew bald, nor gray, nor
wise, as many believed, perhaps justly, having that inconsequence which is fatal to success, yet blessed with that fairy gift held by
few—the power of keeping unbroken, with all
its rainbow hues intact, the bubble of his own
life.

ARETHUSA

ARETHUSA

IN whatever month Arethusa, the nymph
of Elis, fled from her lover Alpheus, the river god, her namesake the flower, pursued and overtaken by her des-
tiny of life, arrived in May. She paused
on the border of the marsh, tremulous in
the soft spring wind, clad in her single
leaf-gown of green, drooping delicately
her lovely head, exhaling her sweet breath
deeply, like one who pants after running,
until it might well have betrayed her presence. But it is seldom that any man
sees the flower arethusa, for she comes
rarely to secluded places, and blooms to
herself. Of all the spring flowers, arethusa
is one of the rarest and the most beautiful
of the great wild orchid family to which
she belongs; she is the maiden. In that
great orchid family are many flowers in
semblances of strange and uncanny things,

of fiends, and elves, and dragons, and un-classed beings, but arethusa comes in the likeness of a fair and delicate nymph. There is about her no horror of the gro-tesque and unnatural, only tender, timid bloom, and maybe a gentle dread of love and a repellent curve of her rosy lip.

Every spring when arethusa appeared there came another maiden to visit her in her shy fastness. She belonged to a family living on the country road, a mile across the fields. It was a rough way to travel, but the girl trod it with the zeal of one friend hastening to see another for the first time after a long absence. She was small and spare, with a thin, rosy-cheeked face, and a close-braided cap of silky dark hair. Everything about the girl except her hair seemed fluttering and blowing. She wore ruffled garments of thin fabrics, and she walked swiftly with a curious movement of her delicate shoulder-blades, almost as if they were propelling her like wings. Her eyes had an intent expression of joyful anticipation and unrestrained impulse of motion. She wore gay-colored gowns—blues, and pinks, and greens—and she was exquisitely dainty. She was an only

"*There came another maiden to visit her*"

daughter, and her mother's chief delight
was to adorn her with fine needle-work.
This needle-work seemed the only fully
opened gate between the mother and the
daughter, for their two natures were so
widely at variance that even love could only
cramp them painfully together. The mother
was a farmer's widow, carrying on a great
farm with a staff of hired men and a farmer.
She was shrewd and emulative, with a
steady eye and ready elbow for her place
in the ranks. The only fineness of detail
about her was her love for dainty needle-
work and her delight in applying it to the
decoration of love. Through the long summer afternoons the mother used to sit beside
her window, plying her needle on fine cam-
brics, and linens, and muslins, and felt
vaguely that by so doing she kept herself
more nearly abreast with the object of her
love and adoration. Sometimes she used
to sigh in a bewildered fashion when she
saw the girl, whose name was Lucy, fluttering away across the field, for she was
to her incomprehensibly fond of long solitary
walks; then she would turn for a solace
to the fine hem of her frock, and so seem to
follow at a little distance. As for the girl,

when she danced away across the fields, a curious sense of flight from she knew not what was always over her. Her heart beat fast. She half amused, half terrified herself with the sound of imaginary footsteps behind her. When she reached the green marsh, she felt safe, both from real and imaginary pursuers.

Arethusa stood on the border of the marsh, else the girl could not have penetrated to her hiding-place. Once there, she stooped and looked at her. She bent over her and inhaled her fragrant breath, which seemed to her like a kiss of welcome. She never picked the flower. She never quite knew why she did not.

"There is such a beautiful flower in the swamp now," she told her mother.

"Where is it?" asked her mother.

"Oh, in the swamp."

"Didn't you pick it?"

"Oh no."

"Why didn't you?"

"I don't know."

"Well, Edson will go after supper and get it for you; maybe there are more," said her mother.

"Oh no, no!" the girl cried out, in terror,

"I wouldn't have it picked for anything, mother. It would die then, and it is such a beautiful flower!"

"You are a queer child," her mother said, adoringly but wonderingly.

"Let me try on your new dress now; I can't sew the sleeves in till I do."

When Lucy slipped her thin girlish arms into the ruffled muslin, she cried out with delight. "Why, that is just the color of the flower!" she said.

"You ought to have it to wear with it to the party to-morrow night, then," said her mother.

"Oh, mother, I wouldn't have it picked for anything!" cried Lucy. Lucy did not want to go to the party, though she would not tell her mother so. She was gently acquiescent towards all wishes of others. Indeed, the girl herself seemed but a mild acquiescence towards existence and the general scheme thereof. She had no more vital interest in the ordering of daily village and domestic life than the flower arethusa over in the swamp. With her feet of a necessity in the mould, her head seemed thrust well outside the garden-pale of common life.

She had no real mates among girls of her age. Her mother was anxious that she should have, and had made little parties for her, but from the first, even when she was a child, Lucy had never come out of her corner of gentle aloofness.

When it came to lovers, the girl's beauty and sweetness and prospective property had lured many, but one after another withdrew, strangely discomfited. They might as well have sat on a meadow-stone and wooed a violet as this girl. She was unfailingly sweet, but utterly unresponsive. The village young men began to say that Lucy Greenleaf wasn't as smart as some. They could explain in no other way her lack of comprehension of that untaught but self-evident language of love and passion in which they had addressed her.

However, when Edson Abbot came, he was persistent, both because he was incredulous as to any girl being unlike other girls, and because he always seized with a grip, which made his own fate, upon anything which seemed about to elude him.

"I wish she would fancy you, Edson, but I'm afraid it isn't any use," Mrs. Greenleaf told him.

"A girl's fancy depends mostly upon a man's," he replied, "and I can hold my fancy to the wheel longer than some men. I shouldn't have given up like Willy Slosum."

"It isn't so much because she won't as because she neither won't nor will," said her mother, with a sigh of bewilderment. This woman, who had been insensibly trained by all her circumstances of life to regard a husband like rain in its season, or war, or a full harvest, or an epidemic, something to be accepted without question if offered, whether good or bad, as sent by the will of the Lord, and who had herself promptly accepted a man with whom she was not in love, without the least hesitation, and lived as happily as it was in her nature to live ever after, could not possibly comprehend the nature of her own daughter.

She was, moreover, with that passionate protectiveness which was the strongest feature of her mother-love, anxious to see this little ewe lamb of hers well settled in life with some one to shield her from its storms before she herself was taken from her. Edson Abbot, the young man who took charge of the farm and lived with

153

them, entirely filled her ideal of what Lucy's husband should be. He was handsome, with a strong masculine description of good looks which appealed to her powerfully. He came of a fine family, but treated the tillage of the earth from a scientific stand-point. He had books and papers about, which were as Greek to Mrs. Greenleaf, but which impressed her still more with his unusual ability to take care of her darling.

"I don't want to hurry you, Lucy," she said to her daughter one day. "I know you ain't very strong, but Edson is one man in a thousand, and it doesn't seem right for you to let him slip through your fingers, just for want of a kind word. You don't pay any more attention to him than you do to that strange bush at the gate."

Lucy looked at her mother, then at the syringa-bush standing, all clothed in white like a bride, at the gate.

"What do you want me to do, mother?" she asked.

"Do, child? Why, treat Edson Abbot the way any other girl in this town would treat him, and give all her old shoes for the chance."

154

"'Do you mean for me to kiss him?'"

The soft red mounted slowly over the girl's face, as she still looked at her mother.

"Do you mean for me to kiss him?" whispered she. "I don't feel as if I could."

A swift blush came over the older woman's face. She laughed, half in embarrassment, half in dismay. "I never saw such a baby in my life as you be," said she; "will you never be anything but a baby, Lucy? It scares me to think of leavin' you some day, if you ain't different. *You* ain't fit to take care of yourself, and Edson is a good man, and he thinks a heap of you, and mother wants to make sure you're taken care of—that's all. Don't you feel as if you might be willing to marry Edson some time if he asked you, Lucy?"

The girl shook and trembled, and eyed her mother with a strange intentness as of fascinated fear. "Oh, mother, I don't want to," she said. "I don't want to marry anybody. I don't like men. I am afraid of them. I want to stay with you."

"You can stay with me. You can go right on living with me, dear child. You shall never leave mother as long as she lives, and she will never leave you."

"I want to just live with you," said Lucy;
"I don't like men."

"Girls are apt to feel that way," said
her mother, "but you'd come to feel different after a while. It's the way people
were meant to do; to be married and given
in marriage. You know what it says in
the Bible. And then you would be sure
to have somebody to take care of you as
long as you live."

"Wouldn't I have God?" asked Lucy,
with an indescribably innocent rounding of
her soft eyes at her mother.

"God sends people to take care of folks,"
replied her mother, judicially. "He can't
come down to earth and see to it that your
fires are kindled, and your paths shovelled
out, and your wood chopped, and all the
heavy things of life lifted off your shoulders.
Think of the way Susan Dagget lives."

Lucy was unconvinced and unmoved by
all this reasoning. She was much more
convinced by the steady broadside of a
strong masculine will brought skilfully
to bear upon her at all times and seasons.
Edson Abbot was a most able young man,
of great strength of character, and even
some talent. He was something of a dip-

lomat in his wooing. He never frightened
this fine, timid creature, who never looked
at him without the impulse of flight in her
eyes, like a rabbit or a bird. He was exceedingly gentle, but she was made to feel
always his firm, unrelaxing will towards
her, and his demand for her obedience.
Whenever he saw that his presence was
awakening beyond control the wild impulses which always underlie timidity, he
pressed her no further; he withdrew, but
when she needed him he was always there.

Insensibly, she began to depend upon
him for services which had always come
from her mother. Then he had a ready skill
to invent some of his own. It was Edson
who conceived the idea of a wild garden for
her in a corner of the field, who had a minia-
ture pond of lilies made for her for a birth-
day surprise. Lucy acquired the habit of
looking at him as she had always looked
at her mother for confirmation and encouragement. He humored her in all her little
idiosyncrasies. When her mother feared
to have her take a long, solitary ramble,
since a tramp had been seen in the neighborhood, he took her part and bade her
go, and himself followed, unseen, at a dis-

tance to protect her. She came gradually to think of him as always on her side, even against her own mother. When one day he again asked her to marry him, though she still looked at him with flight in her eyes, she listened. He pleaded well, for, although he wondered at himself, he loved this slight, frail girl, who, in comparison with others of her age and time, seemed either to have scarcely arrived upon the same level or to have passed it.

Edson got no answer to his suit that night, but the next, coming home from the village, he saw a white flutter at the gate, and Lucy came slowly down the road to meet him. It was the first time such a thing had happened. It was full moonlight, and he could see her face quite plainly when she reached him and paused. It expressed the utmost gentleness and docile assent; only her body, which still shrank away from him, and her little hands, which she kept behind her like a child who will not yield up some sweet, betrayed anything of her old alarm. "I will," she said, tremulously; "I will, Edson. Mother says I ought to, and I will."

It was not a very flattering acceptance

of a lover's suit, but if the grasp of possession be strong enough it precludes the realization of any lack of pressure on the other hand. Edson found no fault with it. His heart seemed fairly to leap forward and encompass the girl, but he no more dared touch her than he would have touched a butterfly which had settled upon his hand. He could always keep a straight course on the road to his own desires. "You shall never regret it, darling," he said, and so controlled his voice, even then, that only a look of startled wonder came into the girl's eyes. Then she walked home with him contentedly enough, fluttering along at his side. There was undoubtedly something about the love and tenderness of this handsome, strong fellow which pleased her after a fashion. She had something in common with others of her sex. She might be cold, if such a negative state could be called cold, but she loved, or she had not dwelt on the earth at all. It was only when he pursued her too ardently that she rebelled.

Edson and Lucy went in to the girl's mother, who began to cry when she saw them coming. "Oh, you dear child; mother is so glad," she said, and held Lucy closely and kissed her.

After Mrs. Greenleaf had gone to bed, the young man and the girl sat side by side on the door-step in the moonlight. Her little hands were folded in her lap. He looked longingly at them.

Suddenly Lucy spoke, fixing her child-like eyes fully upon his face.

"I found that beautiful flower, for the first time this year, to-day in the swamp," said she.

"What flower, sweet?" Edson asked, and took advantage of the unwariness of her thoughts to lay his hand over hers, which fluttered a little.

"Ought I to let you hold my hand because you are going to marry me?" said she.

"Of course. Go on. What was the flower, darling?"

"That beautiful flower that comes every spring, you know."

"Did you bring it home?"

"Bring it home! No, I wouldn't pick it for anything in the world."

"I'll get you some to-morrow; I guess I know the flower you mean. The swamp is too wet for you to go far. I will find a whole bouquet of those flowers for you."

Lucy pulled her hand away fiercely. "If—if you do that, if you pick that flower, I—I will never marry you, Edson Abbot."

The young man laughed, though a little uneasily. For the first time a doubt as to the actual normal mental state of the girl came into his mind, then he dismissed it. She was simply, as he had told himself a hundred times, poetical and ultra-imaginative, a fine elusive moonlight sort of nature, grafted into the shrewd, practical New England stock. She was like a maiden out of a midsummer-night dream, but she was only the more precious for that. "Darling," he said, "I would no more pick that flower, if you did not want me to do so, than I would hurt you."

The marriage was fixed for a year later. Mrs. Greenleaf herself pleaded for time. "She is young, and not strong, Edson," she said. "I think she ought to have time to get used to the idea. Then, too, I want to make her outfit."

Edson yielded easily enough. He himself had doubts as to the wisdom of swift proceeding with Lucy. Then, too, he was ambitious. He was putting in some hot-houses, and he wished to be sure of a larger income before settling himself in matrimony. He had put in some money, and was to work the farm on shares. Mrs. Greenleaf grew prouder than ever of her prospective son-in-law. She was thoroughly happy. She stitched away on Lucy's dainty garments, and every stitch seemed one towards the completion of her own wedding attire. She had never been in love herself, and now that came to her for the first time, through her loving imagination over her daughter. Edson Abbot was the sort of man whom she might herself have loved, and she, being so bound up in unselfish love for the girl, could in a measure grasp all her happiness, and so, in a sense, she grasped her lover.

As for Lucy, she did not seem unhappy. She was peaceful and docile. She sewed a little on her wedding clothes, she went walking and driving with Edson, she sat with him sometimes a little while after her mother had gone to bed; she always smiled readily at him with her sweet, evasive sort of smile. She acquiesced, with the greatest docility, in her mother's suggestion that she should learn something more of house-wifery than she had hitherto known. She spent hours cooking and setting the house in order. She had not done much of that, being delicate, and always shielded by her strong mother; and that had been one of the grounds of complaint against her in the neighborhood. Now, however, she surprised everybody. "She's taken hold as well as anybody I ever see," reported the extra help whom Mrs. Greenleaf had hired Thanksgiving week. "She's real smart. She made as good a plum-puddin' as I ever eat."

Indeed, there seemed to come to the girl an awakening either of latent cleverness or inherited instincts. She seemed to take a certain pleasure in her new tasks, and she thrived under them. She grew stouter; her cheeks had a more fixed color. Abbot was triumphant. He realized less and less that anything was wanting to the sum of his happiness. Such was the force of his own will that, once on the turn towards possession, he comprehended no other coun-ter-current. The wedding-day was fixed in the month of May. The ceremony was to take place at eight o'clock in the evening. When that hour came all the guests were assembled, the bridegroom, bridesmaids, and minister were waiting, but the bride had disappeared. Her wedding-gown lay on her bed with her veil; her little white shoes stood prettily toed out side by side, but the bride was gone. Her mother and Edson conferred in Lucy's chamber.

"They mustn't know it, if we can find her without it," said Mrs. Greenleaf. Her face was white and set; she jerked her black-silk elbow towards the floor, indicating the company assembled below. Edson looked palely at her. "Where do you think she is?" he said.

"I don't know. I've looked everywhere. She ain't in the house."

For once Edson Abbot seemed dazed. He stared at Mrs. Greenleaf.

"You don't think—" he began.

"I don't know but we've made a mistake," said the woman, brokenly. "I don't know as Lucy ought to have had anybody but her mother."

Then the young man made an impatient exclamation. "It is too late to talk about that now," he said. "I'm going to find her."

He strode out of the chamber and down

the back stairs, lest the company see him. The sound of their voices floated after him as he slipped out of the house. He did not know where to begin his search, but some instinct took him into the field behind the house. He hastened across it, a handsome, stalwart figure in his wedding-suit. His face was pale, his brows bent; he felt as if he had met a wall of gossamer with a shock of alabaster. The utter docility and gentleness of the girl made this frightful. He felt no alarm for her safety. He seemed to understand that she had set herself against him in a last assertion of her maiden freedom.

The sun was low in an ineffable rosy sky, with dregs of violet at the horizon line. One great star was burning through the paling radiance. A fragrant, damp coolness was rising from the earth; a silvery film of dew was over all the grass. He heard in the distance the sound of a cow-bell and a boy whistling. All these familiar sights and sounds served to enrage this man whose feet were set so firmly in the regular tracks of life still further with this savor of the irregular and the unusual which had come to him. He felt for the first time a fierce impulse to bend forcibly this other will which had come into contact with his own. He thought, with a sort of fury, of all those waiting people. Then he saw coming towards him across the field, with her singular half-flying motion of the shoulders and arms, the girl whom he was seeking.

He strode forward rapidly to meet her, and grasped her roughly by her slender arm. "Lucy, what does this mean?" he asked, frowning down at her sternly.

She looked at him with such terror that it intimidated him more than any defiance could have done. He weakened, for, after all, he loved her.

"Lucy," he said, gently, "you should not have gone off like this. Don't you know what time it is?"

"Is it eight yet?" she gasped.

"Of course it is, and after."

"I thought I had time," she faltered.

"Time for what?"

"To see if that flower had come. I thought if it had, it would be gone before we get back. I thought I had time, Edson."

"You ought to have picked that flower just this once to wear to your wedding, you think so much of it," said Mrs. Greenleaf.

"Oh, mother!" said Lucy.

"The last assertion of her maiden freedom"

"You are a queer child," her mother said, laughing in an odd, embarrassed fashion. Along with her great tenderness towards this little ewe lamb of hers, she felt that night a singular awe and shame and wonder, almost as if she herself stood in her place.

When Lucy, in her bridal array, went downstairs, people drew long breaths.

"She looks like an angel," one woman whispered, so loud that many heard her. There was, in fact, that about the girl's beauty, as she floated among them in her bridal white, which made her seem more than human. She apparently did not realize that the eyes of all the company were upon her. She stood beside her bridegroom before the minister as unconscious as arethusa over yonder in the swamp. A color as purely fine as the flower's was in her cheeks; in her eyes were as mysterious depths of sweetness.

"She looked as handsome as a picture," the neighbors said, going home when the wedding was over and the bridal pair had departed. "But she don't look quite right, somehow. Wonder what made her so late?" They further mentioned this and that girl who, in their estimation, would have made a more reliable helpmeet than Lucy Greenleaf.

However, Lucy seemed, as time went on, to prove them mistaken. She filled her place as wife and mother well to all appearances. There were two handsome children, with Edson's sturdy beauty. They bore not the slightest resemblance to their mother. "They are all Edson's," Mrs. Greenleaf used to say. Lucy loved them, and they loved her, yet they went from the first more naturally to their father and grandmother.

"They act more like your children than your daughter's," the neighbors said. "Lucy takes good care of them," her mother returned, jealously. That was quite true. Lucy neglected nothing and nobody. She performed all her duties with a fine precision. She seemed happy, yet always she had that look of her youth, the look of one who, with her feet on the common earth, can see past common horizons. And every spring she went by herself, when she could, stealing away unnoticed, to see that great orchid in bloom in the swamp for the first time that year. She never allowed her children to follow her; if the little things tried to do so, she sent them back. Her husband also forbade them, indulging, as he had always done, his wife in what he considered a harm-

less idiosyncrasy, not dreaming that it had
its root in the very depths of her nature, and
that she perhaps sought this fair neutral
ground of the flower kingdom as a refuge
from the exigency of life. In his full tide
of triumphant possession he was as far from
the realization of the truth as was Alpheus,
the fabled river god, after he had overtaken
the nymph Arethusa, whom, changed into
a fountain to elude his pursuit, he had followed under the sea, and never knew that,
while forever his, even in his embrace, she
was forever her own.

Every spring this woman, growing old as
to her fair, faded face, went to see arethusa,
coming upon her standing on the border of
the marsh, clad in her green leaf, drooping
delicately her beautiful purplish-pink head,
with the same rapture as of old. This soul,
bound fast to life with fleshly bonds, yet forever maiden, anomalous and rare among her
kind, greeted the rare and anomalous flower
with unending comfort and delight. It was
to her as if she had come upon a fair rhyme
to her little halting verse of life.

MOUNTAIN-LAUREL

MOUNTAIN-LAUREL

LADD'S MOUNTAIN was to the east-
ward of the village, consequently the
sun rose behind it. When the full radiance
crowned it at last, the dewy depths of the
shadows were revealed; great mysterious
lights as of the very watch-fires of the day
gleamed out, and here and there silver
threads of mountain torrents dazzled as
with diamonds. But the laurel, of course,
could not be seen from the village; only to
the farer in the mountain-ways were its
gorgeous thickets displayed. There was
a marvellous growth of it on Ladd's Mountain. Young people used to make parties
to climb the mountain, and go home laden
with great bunches of the superb chintz-
patterned blossoms. In the winter its
glossy evergreen leaves were in high demand for Christmas wreaths and decora-
tions. But Samuel Ladd was the one who set

the greatest value upon it. It had reached for him its highest beauty, being more to him than itself, and having, in a sense, flowered out beyond its own natural scope, in a far-reaching influence upon a human soul.

Samuel Ladd actually owned the mountain, and was land-poor in the fullest sense. Formerly a wide stretch of fertile meadows on the river-bank below had belonged to his family; now only the mountain remained. There was scarcely an acre of hay or pasturage on its rocky sides. Even the wood was of scanty growth and undesirable kinds. There was more laurel than anything else on Ladd's Mountain.

The Ladd house was half-way up the southern slope of the mountain, where the rough road ended and the rougher path to the summit began. The house stood on a narrow level of cultivated fields, a natural terrace of the mountain. There Samuel Ladd had been born, and there he had lived his whole life; he was nearly forty years old. He had been one of a large family—six brothers and three sisters— but every one was gone. Only the two oldest sisters had lived until middle life.

They — two round - shouldered, hopeless, patient - faced women — died of consumption when Samuel was in his twenties. After that he lived alone, except during the busy season of the year, when he hired help from the village. Although a young man, he never sought companions. He never cared for any of the village merry-makings. Through the long winter evenings and the long storms he remained alone over his one fire, listening to the shrieking of the mountain wind around the old farm-house, but he was never, in the fullest sense, lonely. He possessed an imagination that, joined to the other qualities of brain needful, might have made him a great poet. To this man none of his family were really dead, but lived in a sublimated and wonderful fashion. His father's poor body lay in the graveyard over in the village, but in his stead sat, for the son's fancy, in his old place beside the hearth, a splendid, stalwart figure, radiant with the enjoyment of life; and instead of the feeble and worn mother was a grand creature as full of strength and grace as a mountain pine. And the two round-shouldered women, his sisters, who had dragged away their loveless lives in this mountain solitude, reappeared to the fair fancy of their young brother in all their lost loveliness and hope of youth. Samuel never imagined them as they had really been but always as they might have been had time and trouble not touched them. One might have wondered if the boy, through his affection, had always seen his lost dear ones as he afterwards pictured them to himself, and had actually never realized their true aspects in other eyes.

On moonlight nights in summer, as he sat peacefully on the step of the door overlooking the valley, seeing the village below as through the waves of a shifting silver flood, his beautiful young sisters used to come and sit beside him, and, as they talked together, Samuel's sisters were much more companions for him dead than when living, since he was so at liberty to reanimate them into accord with himself. In life, they had paid little attention to their younger brother. They had had their whole strength taken and exhausted by their treadmill of narrow duties, and the slow grinding of their hearts on the wheel of disappointment of the main ends of life. They had become breathing

anities of women, neither kind nor unkind,
either gloomy nor cheerful, sunken into
s stupidly selfish regard of their own
anding and feeding places as cows. But
amuel had invested them both, when they
ere gone, and, maybe, when they were
ill drudging along their narrow paths
 earth, with such garments of glory that
ey had not known themselves in them,
ot even in their dim orthodox imagina-
ons of their future harped and winged
states. Their brother made of them shapes
ifinitely more desirable than those of their
wn conception, and transcended, as love can
ften do, their dreams even of their own
ood.

When, one day some ten years after his
ast sister had died, a party of young people
ame up the mountain, and among them
as a strange young girl, such a beauty
nat people turned to look after her, Samuel
stonished the man who was working for
im that summer by remarking that that
irl looked like his sister Eunice.

"What?" cried the man, with an in-
redulous stare. He was a young fellow
f about Samuel's age, full of stolid energy
ke an ox. He was a good farm-hand,

and was earning enough money to buy a farm in the village and marry.

"She looks as my sister Eunice used to," said Samuel.

"Your sister Eunice? Good Lord!" cried the man. "Your sister Eunice? Why, your sister Eunice was as thin as a lath, and stooped till she was most double, and her skin was yellow as saffron, and her eyes like a fish's! That girl look like your sister Eunice You're stun-blind, Sammy."

Samuel gazed at the girl, who was seated with her companions on the stone wall across the road, resting before they began the harder part of the ascent. He compared her laughing eyes, her sweet, rosy cheeks and lips, her yellow hair, her lovely young shoulders, with his memory of his poor dead sister's, and, wrought upon by some divine alchemy of love, he found the same likeness as before. "I should almost take her for Eunice, if I didn't know," he said, with mild persistency.

"You're a fool," said the hired man.

Samuel made no reply; he was meditating, his forehead knitted over his deep-set, pale-blue eyes. When the party had left their resting-place on the stone wall, and had disappeared up the mountain-path, he went promptly into the house.

"Ben't you goin' to turn that hay?" the hired man called after him, wonderingly.

"No," said Samuel, gently but decisively. The hired man stood staring a moment, after the door closed behind Samuel, then he whistled and slouched off to the hay-field at the right of the house.

When the little party returned, Samuel was dressed in his best; he had shaved and brushed his long, sallow locks, he had put on a clean shirt, with an obsolete, rasping collar, and a tie which his sister Eunice had made for him out of a piece of her black-silk dress. His suit was one which had belonged to his father, and it hung in loose folds on his lank figure. Besides all this, Samuel wore in his button-hole a sprig of mountain-laurel. The long-unused parlor was open, and the paper curtains flapped in the wind like flowered green sails. The hired man out in the field saw them blowing, and made an errand around to the front of the house to get a drink of water from the well in the yard. He gulped it down, with long stares over the brim of the dipper. When he passed the parlor windows, he cast a shrewd and comprehensive stare at the interior and went on, whistling again. Samuel had set a great glass pitcher of milk on the mahogany card-table in the parlor. He had looked forlornly in his bachelor larder for some dainty to accompany the milk, but there was nothing except cold vegetables, a ham-bone, some eggs, and cheese. Then he had searched the cellar, and brought up, triumphantly, two little tumblers of currant-jelly which had survived since his sister Eunice's time. He set these out on the card-table beside the milk, with six of the best china plates, and six teaspoons. After that he hastened out behind the house and broke off branches of the mountain-laurel, which was in full blossom. He filled an old copper-gilt pitcher, which was precious, though he did not know it, with the laurel, and stuck the sprig in his coat. Then he was ready.

He stood on his front door-step when the four girls and the two young men who made up the party reached it. He was flaming with bashfulness, but resolute in his purpose. He invited them all in to have some refreshment. There was a moment's hesitation; the girls stared at him, then at one another, with covert smiles. Samuel Ladd's name had become a synonym in the village for rustic uncouthness and abashedness, and this was unprecedented. Then the beauty, who was a school-teacher from another town, took the lead. She accepted the invitation promptly, and followed Samuel into the house and the best parlor. Covert smiles became, in the case of two hysterical girls, almost open merriment at the sight of the refreshment spread before them, but the school-teacher's manner was perfect.

"How delicious!" she cried; "new milk! And I don't know when I have had any currant-jelly! It is currant-jelly, isn't it, Mr. Ladd? Yes, I thought so."

When the guests left, the school-teacher bore in triumph the beautiful copper-gilt pitcher which she had admired, and which Samuel had urged upon her acceptance. One of the young men carried for her the great bouquet of mountain-laurel. Samuel stood looking after them. He had never been in his whole life so happy after the fashion of other men.

That evening he stole down the mountain to the farm-house at the foot where the school-teacher boarded. He was going courting for the first time in his life. He was dressed in his best; he wore an ancient silk hat which had belonged to his father when a young man, he had a fresh sprig of laurel in his button-hole, and he carried a superb bunch of it.

But just as he reached the gate of the farm-house where the school-teacher boarded an-other man was going up the flower-bordered path to the front door, and he recognized him as one of the party who had climbed the mountain in the afternoon. He was a stran-ger from the city who was in the village on some engineering business.

Samuel waited in the shadow of a bush at the gate until the other man had been admit-ted, then he turned away, but not before Mrs. Cutting, the woman of the house, had espied him. She was crossing the road from the field with a basket of greens, and she hailed him. "Hullo, Samuel!" said she; "couldn't you get in? The school-teacher is there. I should have thought she would have gone to the door. Did you knock?" Samuel stood before the woman, and he seemed to be settling down into his very boots with an abashedness which was almost ignominy. "I guess I won't go in," said he. "I guess she's got company."

Mrs. Cutting laughed significantly.

"Well, mebbe you'd better not, if *he's* come,"

said she. "It's Mr. Crane, I s'pose. He's payin' attention to her. He comes every night. Mebbe you'd better not go in—still, as long as you've come—"

"I guess I won't go in," replied Samuel, with a pathetic, breathless kind of dignity. He was quite pale. He extended the great bunch of laurel. "Mebbe you'll give her these flowers by-and-by, when he's gone," said he.

"Land!" cried the woman, "she's got a bunch as big as my head now. I don't see what she can do with any more. But she'll be jest as much obliged to you, Samuel."

"All right," said Samuel.

Samuel went up the mountain with his despised offering of laurel. When he reached the terrace upon which his house stood, he paused and looked down over the valley, the cultivated fields and gardens, the river, and the white village beyond, all wavering under the silver film of moonlight into outlines of imaginary beauty. "Seems to me I never knew this house stood so high," he muttered. Without knowing it, he had reached a new spiritual outlook, and even a material landscape seemed farther beneath his material mountain.

There was still a pained expression on his face when he entered his house, but it vanished at once. A moonbeam lay athwart the kitchen floor, and in it stood, white and fair, and radiant with smiles, beautiful beyond her utmost compass of pretty youthfulness, the same girl who was at that moment sitting with her lover in the farm-house in the valley.

"Lord, I forgot that," said Samuel Ladd. "I can always have her this way as long as I live."

Presently the few people who came up the mountain wondered what had started Samuel Ladd fixing up his house. He took a little hoard from the savings-bank, put the old place in perfect repair, and made some improvements. There was a new portico at the front door, with a climbing-rose trained over it; lace curtains swayed at the parlor windows. People began to surmise that Samuel Ladd was going to get married, but they were at a loss for the bride. None of them dreamed that the man had refurnished his house, not for a bride, but for a home for the most precious imagination of his soul. And the refurnishing did not extend to his house alone, for ever afterwards he was dainty, even to punctiliousness, in his attire. No man in the village wore more carefully brushed and mended clothes, or was more religiously shaven, and that, although he lived days and weeks on his solitary farm with no human eye to look upon him.

The pretty school-teacher did not return after the close of the spring term. She married the young engineer, and went to live in a distant city. Samuel saw the notice of her marriage in the paper; he cut it out and pasted it on a fly-leaf of his copy of *Paradise Lost*. He hesitated awhile between that and the Bible, but finally decided in favor of the former. Samuel had a small assortment of books, mostly of a religious character, with the exception of a history of Massachusetts. He cared especially for the Bible and the Milton. The Milton he pored over for hours at a time, but mostly for purposes of comparison after he began to write himself, which he did soon after the school-teacher left the village. This pretty, usual girl became, without knowing it, in a humble, almost ludicrous, fashion, a species of Laura to this rustic, inglorious Petrarch. Almost simultaneously with Samuel Ladd's love there awakened within him that desire which has from all time awakened in such wise—to achieve and succeed and win fame for love's sake. This male of his species had found, along with his love, his song, albeit it was a poor and discordant one. He looked at the laurel bushes, and a faint conception of their eternal symbolism came to him. He had no creative talent, so he followed the one poet whom he knew, afar off, with pompous halts and hitches of imitation. He filled reams of foolscap with trite sentiments and weighty platitudes, in a babel of strange rhymes and sonorous syllables and swollen metres. Samuel was fond of marching up and down, either in his orchard or his parlor, and mouthing his own poetry with solemn emphasis, his hands clasped rigidly behind his back. Sometimes his hired man used to overhear him, and stand aloof and listen, grinning. Gradually the report spread that Samuel Ladd wasn't quite in his right mind, though he seemed sane enough in all his business dealings. Occasionally the young people passing the house on their way to the summit used to hear Samuel declaiming, and

"The Milton he pored over"

stopped and stared and nudged one another. These young creatures, travelling along the common track of daily life, with all its wayside weeds as giant trees to their per- spectives, saw much to jest at in the pain- ful and futile efforts of this poor brother to raise himself above their level. When he fell back, or thought himself above when he was still below, they were keen to see the absurdity of it, being themselves ac- curately balanced to detect any eccentricity of orbit. However, they were kind to him. Often they used to stop, on their way down the mountain, and leave the remnants of their luncheons for the poor old bachelor with no woman to cook the village dainties for him. Samuel was fond of presenting them, in return, with copies of his poems.

Samuel never essayed the publication of his poems in a legitimate fashion by a pub- lisher. He spent all his little savings, and went without necessary food, to have them printed at his own expense, in paper-covered volumes, by a local printer. These he used to give away; he never sold them — he was above that. He went about the village leav- ing the book at the doors, and it was the proudest day of his whole life. He knew of nothing wanting, not even the girl whom he loved. He was conscious of possessing something beyond her, which still included her—that which he had made of himself for her sake.

One May, long after the pretty school-teacher had married and gone away, she came back to the village, and one afternoon she joined a party for climbing the mountain and gathering laurel. Samuel, sitting in his doorway, saw her, and never knew her; and she had forgotten him. She had grown old, and all her pretty individualities, her diamond facets of character, had been rubbed smooth into utter commonness by the friction of an utterly common life. Her youthful bloom had gone, and something more—the essential perfume which had crowned and winged the bloom. Samuel looked at her as she passed, then he turned away; and she looked at him, and turned away also.

"That's Samuel Ladd," said a woman at her side. "He writes poetry; he's sort of crazy."

"He looks queer," assented the other. She had seen neither Samuel as he was, nor beside him her own glorified image, that self to which she could never attain on earth, fade-

less in transcendent youth, while she, coarse
and common, passed on. Samuel held a
volume of his poems in his hand; he had
been reading them aloud to himself. Utter
dross though they might be, they had yet not
failed in the mission of perfect art. They
had filled a soul with the conviction of work
well done and the elation of success. After
all, the worker is more than the work, and he
who does his best with poor tools may crown
himself with genuine laurels.

Samuel had planted laurel closely around
his house, and his windows were almost hidden by it. All Samuel's rooms were, summer and winter, in a green twilight with the
laurel, as was perhaps his mind. He loved
it at all times, but especially in its blooming
season as now.

Between those great bushes, resplendent
with their white and rosy stars and evergreen
leaves, sat the poor poet and lover, who had
fed all his life upon the honey in his own soul
in lieu of any other, and perhaps nourished
himself to his own waste, but to his own happiness. No happier soul was there in the
valley below, no happier soul ever came May-
ing up the mountain-side. Sitting there beneath the shade of his splendid symbolic

flowers, with his fadeless ideal to wife, and his consciousness of an artist soul invincible by any poverty of art, he was one of the happiest crowned heads in the world.

PEONY

PEONY

THE peony returned with the rose to
her old haunt in the garden. The
garden was in the front yard; the long
rectangle on either side of the front walk
was laid out in box-bordered beds of flowers,
prominent among which were the roses
and the peonies. The roses were the old-
fashioned kinds—great single red and white
ones and blushing-roses. The peonies were
themselves exaggerated copies of the roses,
like coarse country wenches following in the
track of the queen, clad in a tawdry, flaunt-
ing imitation of her fine, royal splendor.
They, too, were colored red and a delicate
rose and white, and their great petals curved
like the rose's, but they had nothing of her
subtle fragrance. However, Arabella Lambert did not believe that. To her the strong
sweetness of the rose-colored and the white
ones, and the simple odor of the red, full of

N 193

the healthy virility of the flower, was much finer than the scent of the rose.

She was fond of plunging her face into the great inflorescence of color, and inhaling with loud sniffs of rapture. "Folks that want to smell of roses, can," she was wont to say. "Roses to me are sickish, and apt to give a head-cold. To my mind, the peony goes far beyond them, and it is enough sight handsomer flower, too. Roses is short-lived, and apt to be eat by rose-bugs. Look at them blushing-roses; it's seldom they ever blow out perfect; but look at the peonies!"

The neighbor to whom she was descanting would profess admiration, if she were given to polite concealment of her own views, but her outside comment would be different. "No wonder Arabella Lambert likes peonies better than roses," she said; "she's as coarse as one. Arabella is dreadful coarse; she always was."

All around Arabella lived extreme types of her countrywomen, thin and pale, with closely shut, thin lips, delicately sharp chins and noses, and high, narrow foreheads, from which the hair was strained back with fierce pulls of nervous, veinous hands. They looked like ascetics, and

were, nourishing their souls only on un-
watered and unsweetened doctrines and
laws, and their bodies on bread and pastry.
In them the fine and intense strain of New
England obtained in full force. They were
delicate, yet more enduring than their sturdy
husbands and sons. The women in the village always outlived the men. Some of
these women had lived so long and worked
so hard that they seemed like automatons,
kept in motion by some past effort of the
will. They were the survival of the type
of women who had breasted the early hard-
ships of the country; their bodies were
getting thin, but they endured through
the might of that strong essence of spirit
within them.

To such women as these Arabella Lambert was an anachronism, belonging to another time and type. She was as foreign as
if she had been born at the antipodes. This
great, overblown, rosy, easy, sensuous creature, who never cared whether she spent or
saved, who never cared, nor even knew,
whether her house was swept and garnished
or not, who did not even seem much concerned as to the salvation of her immortal
soul, was to them a perpetual scandal and

rock of offence. Then, too, her lack of self-repression, her exuberance of emotion before every stress of life, whether of joy or sorrow, shamed them with a curious vicarious shame. They blushed as they spoke in mortified whispers of this or that which Arabella Lambert had said or done.

But Arabella herself never dreamed of their state of mind, and, if she had, would never have been disturbed by it. Her own life was enough for this woman, and yet it was an exceedingly simple life, consisting of little more than the simplest and most primitive delights. Arabella loved dearly to sit on her door-step, in the shade of her green-hooded porch, and doze; she loved to sleep all night in her high feather-bed in the south chamber; she loved to eat some simple fare which did not require much labor to prepare; she loved to potter around her flower-garden; and she loved to give things away. Arabella was as prodigal of her belongings as the peony out in the yard of its bloom. She had no power of reserve, whether of herself or her earthly possessions. When an afflicted neighbor came to her with an account of her trials, Arabella gave way to such wild sympathy of grief that the woman was abashed and alarmed, and turned comforter herself; and she gave so lavishly to tramps that they avoided the house, thinking she was crazy. Arabella lived alone in a fine old house filled with a goodly store of furniture still, though it had been considerably diminished. Arabella had had some money in the bank, but she had given most of it away. She had never married, and it was confidently believed that she had never had a chance. As one woman astutely remarked, if any man had ever asked Arabella to marry him, she would have felt so badly to say no that she would have had him whether she had wanted him or not. Arabella was believed never to have refused any living creature anything which she had the power to give, and she had had ample opportunities.

Though Arabella had no nearer relatives than one niece, her sister's daughter, she had a host of far-away ones. This tender heart had been besieged for years by an army of cousins, twice and thrice removed, and especially the Stebbinses. Years before, Arabella's second cousin Maria had married a Stebbins. He had at the time four children by a former marriage, and Maria two. From this marriage came four more children. Now the three sets of children had long ago married and had families, and there had been few deaths, consequently the Stebbins family, with ramifications, numbered a multitude. Strangers were bewildered by the number of Stebbinses in the village. Most of them were in straitened circumstances, if not actually needy, and they made the most of Arabella, though they met with one obstacle in the shape of her niece, who was a smart, sharp, single woman, a school-teacher in a town seven miles distant. This niece had some property of her own and was earning a good salary, and so was herself in no need of Arabella's assistance. She kept as sharp a watch as possible that her aunt should not be robbed by her impecunious relatives. She used to say much about it to Arabella. "You know, Aunt Arabella," she would say, "that you have not enough yourself to give so much. One of these days you will be stranded without a cent, and nobody will thank you for it. There is no sense in your giving so much."

"Erastus Stebbins has been real sick and not able to work, Sarah," the old woman replied, "and Abby Ann came over here and cried."

"Let her cry," replied the niece. She had a delicate face which could be pitiless.

"She felt dreadful bad," said Arabella, and she wiped her own eyes, overflowing at the recollection.

"I'd die before I'd come crying to anybody," said the niece; "but that isn't all. You gave away all the wood on the south wood lot to Sam Stebbins last week, Aunt Arabella."

"I had to, I really had to, Sarah," replied Arabella, eagerly. "Samuel's son Billy, he'd been and signed a note, and couldn't get enough money to pay, and Sam, he had to help him out, and it took every cent he had, and they were actually suffering for wood. They actually were, Sarah, and there was Billy's wife with that little baby."

"Let them suffer, then. Better to suffer than to steal."

"Oh, Sarah, it wasn't stealing."

"Yes, it was. The door of your heart is always open, and they walk in and take advantage of it," returned Sarah, stoutly.

"But they would have suffered, Sarah— Billy's wife and that little baby."

UNDERSTUDIES

"Let them suffer; it doesn't hurt people to suffer."

"But you wouldn't want that little baby to freeze, Sarah?"

"I guess they could have kept that little baby warm without stealing your wood," replied Sarah, contracting her lips.

She had come over to spend a week of her vacation with her aunt, her school having closed earlier than usual on account of the measles. The next week she was to visit a cousin; then she was going on an excursion to the mountains. "You had better go with me, Aunt Arabella," she said, presently. "It would do you good, and it isn't going to cost much—only twenty-five dollars—and we can be gone ten days. Lottie White, the grammar-school teacher, is going with me, and you could go, too, just as well as not."

Arabella laughed. Her enormous bulk quite filled up the doorway where she sat. Sarah was in a straight chair on the porch beside her. Arabella gave a facetious glance at the swelling slant, unbroken by any waistline, which swept from under her double chin to her widely planted feet in their cloth slippers. "I'd look pretty climbing mountains, wouldn't I?" said she. Then she laughed

"'I'd look pretty climbing mountains, wouldn't I?'"

again, a hoarsely sweet chuckle disturbing the depths of her great body.

Sarah did not laugh in response. She had not a quick sense of humor. Other people's laughter puzzled her much more than their deeds. She could discover motives for everything else with greater success. ' You would not have to climb, of course," she replied, gravely. "You could ride everywhere. Of course, you could not climb mountains, Aunt Arabella."

"Well, I guess I couldn't go, anyway. I'm just as much obliged to you for thinkin' of it," said Arabella."

"If it is the money," said Sarah, slowly, "I must say I don't feel right about your going without things to give to an able-bodied man like Sam Stebbins, but I've got enough, and it's only twenty-five dollars—and—"

"Oh no, thank you; you're real good, Sarah, but I couldn't take it, nohow. I've got the money; it ain't that. It's only because I don't think it's best."

"Why don't you think it is best?" asked the niece, bluntly.

Arabella colored all over her great face of overlapping curves like a rose or a peony.

"There are reasons," said she, with a curious attempt at dignity.

"Well," said Sarah, coldly, "I don't want to pry into your secrets, Aunt Arabella, but I think it would do you good, and I see no sense in your going without everything for the sake of the shiftless, begging Stebbinses."

"Now, Sarah, Eben Stebbins ain't shiftless; nobody ever said he was. He's always worked hard, but he's been dreadful unfortunate. He's had fire and sickness, and he's sick himself. Look how lame he is with the rheumatism, poor man!"

"Well, I wasn't saying anything against Eben Stebbins," admitted Sarah; "but if he comes begging, he's no better than the rest of them—a man begging of a woman!"

"He hasn't, Sarah," Arabella cried, eagerly. "He hasn't said a word, but I know if he has a wheel-chair, he could get around in it. But nobody has said a word about it. That was what I thought I'd use the money for. Poor Eben has had a dreadful hard time, and I'm dreadful sorry for his daughter Minnie, too."

"What about her?"

"Nothing, only she was going to get married to that Leavitt boy, and he'd just got his

nice new little house built, and he had enough
money saved up to buy the furniture, and the
bank he kept it in has failed up, and he's lost
every dollar, and they've got to put off the
weddin'. Eben offered to take them in with
him, but the young man has got to live on
his farm; you know it's three miles out of
the village. Minnie said she didn't mind if
there wasn't any furniture except the little
her father could spare her—he hasn't got
much, you know—but the young feller is real
proud, and says she sha'n't live so, and he
won't borrow. They feel dreadfully about
it, and I should think they would. I've always heard it was a bad sign to put off a
weddin'."

"Well, I don't see what you can do about
it," said Sarah. She looked suspiciously at
her aunt, who fidgeted a little and made an
evasive answer.

"I don't know as I can do anything," said
she, meekly. She was rather afraid of her
niece. She was, on the whole, relieved when
she went away the first of the following week.
She found it very peaceful to sit undisturbed
in her disordered room, and not have Sarah
raising a dust with the broom and making
her move to facilitate the sweeping. She did

not like a way Sarah had of always shutting
the doors. She loved her doors to be open,
and her windows. She felt aggrieved when
Sarah insisted on having the windows on
the sunny side of the house shut, though she
said nothing. The minute Sarah was gone
Arabella waddled about softly and ponder-
ously, flinging wide open doors and windows
to admit anything which chose to enter—
sunshine, winds, flies, stray cats—anything.
Arabella minded nothing, not even bats or
bumble-bees or hornets. She made everything which chose to enter her home welcome,
being instinct with a spirit of hospitality
which included the little as well as the great.
Arabella was no heartier in her welcome to
the minister than to the old ragman to whom
she sold no rags, but with whom she shared
her dinner. It was not very much of a dinner.
Arabella did not get up very elaborate repasts,
but they were plentiful. She boiled vegetables or greens, she had baker's bread, eggs,
and fruit, currants in their season, and apples.
Arabella had quite an orchard. The village
boys had the run of it. It was only through
their generosity, which spared Arabella some
of her own bounty, that she had any apples
from her own orchard. The boys used to

"Arabella had quite an orchard"

pick some for her, and bring them to the
house, and she was exceedingly grateful,
and never once thought that they had dis-
charged any obligation towards herself by
so doing. Once she spoke to one of the boys'
mothers about it, and the woman looked at
her wonderingly. "Why, I don't see that
it is anything for you to thank them for,"
said she. "I told Franky that he and Al-
bert and George ought to go to work and pick
your apples for you, you had been so good
about giving them so many. Franky has
come home with his pockets stuffed day after
day. I shouldn't have thought you would
have had enough to make any pies."

"Oh, I never make any pies; it's too much
work," said Arabella; "and the boys have
been real good. They have brought ever so
many to me. Sometimes I have been afraid
they have robbed themselves."

"Good land!" cried the woman. "Whose
orchard is it?"

When she went home she told her sister
she didn't know as Arabella Lambert was
altogether right.

The village children descended like a flock
of birds upon Arabella's garden, and pillaged
it at their will. They did not seem to care as

much about the peonies as about the other flowers, like roses or pinks. Their mothers told them not to bring those great coarse things home; they were in the way. Arabella was glad it was so. She would have suffered had the children been too free with the peonies; she might have forbidden them. Her one streak of parsimoniousness showed itself in the case of those great fully blown flowers. She used to watch jealously lest the children trample them. The peonies were in bud the week after Sarah went away, and in full blossom the week after that, and they still endured when Sarah came up the walk one afternoon about five o'clock.

Arabella put on her glasses and stared in a bewildered fashion at the straight, slim, genteel figure in the black India silk coming up the box-bordered path. She herself was sitting as usual in her doorway.

"Why, Sarah Bisbee, that ain't you?" cried Arabella, as her niece drew near. There was a note of dismay as well as surprise in her voice. Sarah put down her black-silk parasol carefully before she replied. She never talked while she was doing anything else.

"Yes, it is I, Aunt Arabella," said she. "Are you surprised?"

"Yes, I guess I be a little. I thought you as up to the mountains."

"Well, I expected to be there," replied arah, "but the excursion was given up on ccount of the illness of the gentleman who as to conduct the party. It is postponed r three weeks. So I thought I would come ver here. I thought I would give your ouse a thorough cleaning, and put up some urrant-jelly for you. Then I saw when I as here that some of your sitting-room hairs, and the parlor ones, too, for that matr, needed fixing up. The wood ought to e rubbed. I've got a nice recipe for furniure polish. Then I want to see about the pare-chamber curtains and the bedspread eing done up, too."

Arabella stared at her niece, and her exression of dismay deepened. "I wouldn't other about them, Sarah," said she, frankly. Seems to me I wouldn't. It would be a ood deal of work, and you must be tired ut."

"I am not half so tired when I am doing omething," replied Sarah, firmly. She ade as if to enter, but her aunt Arabella id not move aside to allow her to do so.

"I guess I'll go in and lay aside my bon-

net," remarked Sarah. Still Arabella di
not move.

Sarah looked at her in growing surprise
but she spoke easily enough. "I guess i
you will just move a little, Aunt Arabella,
said she, "then I'll go in."

Arabella did not stir. She sat perfectl
still, filling up the doorway. Her eyes wer
fixed upon a great clump of red peonies be
side the path.

The thought came to Sarah that possibl
her aunt's hearing was failing. She spok
in the loud, clear, imperative voice whic
she used in the school-room. "If you wi
move a little, please, Aunt Arabella," sai
she, "I will go in and lay aside my bonnet."

Arabella did not move. The look of aston
ishment on Sarah's face deepened to alarn
She touched her aunt, leaning over her, an
shook her gently by the shoulders. "Why
Aunt Arabella," she shouted, "what i
the matter? Can't you hear anything
say?

"Yes, Sarah, I hear every word," replie
Arabella, unexpectedly.

"Well, then, why don't you move a littl
and let me go in? I want to take off m
bonnet."

PEONY

Arabella sat immovable, with her eyes riveted upon the clump of peonies.

Then Sarah straightened herself and stood staring at her aunt in consternation and astonishment which almost convulsed her steady face. Arabella wore an old-fashioned muslin covered with a large pattern in purple cross-bars, between which were little bunches of pink roses. This voluminosity of purple muslin over Arabella's bulk filled up the doorway completely with the apparent lightness of a flower. Out of the soft frills of the muslin arose Arabella's creasy neck and her large, rosy, imperturbable face. Nothing could exceed the obstinacy of gentleness and mildness on that face; it was a power of a kind to stop an army. Sarah continued to stare. "Don't you want me to go in, Aunt Arabella?" she asked, finally.

Arabella made no reply, but her face twitched. It was the first time in her whole life that she had ever held the door of her house against her own kith and kin.

"Well," said Sarah, in a high, thin voice that trembled slightly, "if you don't want me to go in your house, perhaps I had better go home, only it is too late for the stage-coach, and if I go to any of the neighbors to stay all night, they may think it strange that I don't stay here."

Arabella made no reply to that. She was afraid of her niece with the unreasoning and uncalculating fear of a child. She held that door, knowing all the time that it was a futile measure, that her niece must finally enter, that the evil day was only postponed.

Sarah stood for a moment longer undecided. Then she gave her bonneted head a toss and straight to the sitting-room windows she went. They were wide open, and the shutters thrown back.

Sarah gave a long look through a window, then she turned to her aunt, who kept her eyes fixed on the clump of peonies as if she found strength and support therefrom.

"There are only that little card-table and the shovel and tongs, and two chairs and a cricket left in the sitting-room," said Sarah.

Arabella said nothing.

Sarah went to a parlor window and raised herself on tiptoe to look therein. Then she turned to her aunt. "*All* the parlor furniture is gone," said she.

Then Arabella spoke. "I knew how you'd feel about it," said she, "and I hated to have you know, but Minnie she came over here and she cried. She didn't think of havin' my furniture, but she cried, and the next morning I got Jonas Tibbets, and he loaded the furniture into his express-wagon and carried it over to the new house."

"*All* the parlor furniture, and almost *all* the sitting-room gone," said Sarah, slowly, as if she were informing herself.

"I never sat in the parlor, and no more than two at a time ever come into the sitting-room, and I can sit on the cricket," said Arabella.

"Have you given them the chamber furniture?"

"Enough to furnish two chambers—that is all, Sarah."

"The spare-chamber furniture, I suppose?"

"Yes, I did. You know I never have any company to stay all night, except you, Sarah; and you know you always like the east room better; that ain't touched."

"Well," said Sarah, grimly, "I sha'n't have to do up the spare-chamber spread and curtains."

"They would have been a sight of work," said Arabella, eagerly.

Sarah stepped forward. "Well," said she, "it was your own furniture, and I suppose you had a right to do what you wanted to with it. When you have given away the roof off your house, and the clapboards and shingles, and the floor-boards, as you'll be sure to do before you die, you can come to my house, I suppose, and I won't sit in the door and keep you out. Now, Aunt Arabella, if that was the reason why you didn't want me to go in, I know now, and there is no reason for keeping me out any longer. If you will move a little now, I'll go in and lay aside my bonnet."

Arabella moved, half rising, and the slim, black silk-clad figure of her niece pressed past her into the house.

Then Arabella sat down again, and a beatific expression was on her face. She looked like a child who had escaped a scolding, and was radiant and triumphant in the supremacy of its own way, and beyond that look was another, which comes only to the face of the giver, out of all the faces of earth.

She sat there filling up the doorway with her vast bulk, overspread with waves of purple-barred muslin, a woman with no

PEONY

fine development of imagination or intellect, a woman whose whole scheme of existence was on lines so simple that they were fairly coarse, like those of the peony beside the gate, in which the mystery of the rose was lost in the grossness of utter revelation. She only knew enough to bloom like the flower, whether to her own grace or glory it mattered not, so long as it was to her farthest compass, and to yield unstintingly all her largess of life to whomsoever crossed her path with a heart or hand of need for it.

MORNING-GLORY

MORNING-GLORY

ALL over the stone wall in front of the Bemis house the morning - glories thrived, and not only there, but on the trellis-work over the east door. They even trailed along the ground their garlands of purple, and rosy, and white blossoms, when support failed them. The morning-glory prefers a prop for her tender growth, but such is her rapture of youth and morning that she blossoms anywhere. From the face of the rock, from the depths of the dewy grass, from tree, and trellis, prone in the dust of the highway at the mercy of the feet of men, the morning - glories shout out their great silent chorus of triumph through a hundred trumpets of delicate bloom.

The morning-glories had always been a distinctive feature of the Bemis place. Madam Bemis, as she was called, was very fond of them. Madam Bemis was the daughter of

217

old Squire Bemis, and she had married her own cousin, the son of Minister Bemis. Now, squires were out of date, and even ministers of as many years' settlement as her husband's father had lost prestige, but there was still recognition on the part of the villagers for the descendants of such notables, hence the "Madam Bemis." They were emulous of her notice, and they had a pride which was like feudal loyalty in Alexander.

Alexander's father had died when he was a child too young to remember him clearly. The little boy always had a face appear to his mental vision whenever the dead man's name was mentioned, but whether it was true or not he never knew. This vision was not in the least like a portrait of his father, done crudely in oil, which hung in the best parlor. This portrait represented his father as a very young boy, with a face as puffed out with a wind of innocent gayety as a cherub's. He was dressed in the artlessly grotesque fashion of a former generation, in an awkward little nankeen suit, with a wide frill around the neck, and strapped shoes. "I could never see the least resemblance to your father after he was grown up, in that portrait," Alexander's mother used to say; "but I suppose he

must have been like that when he was a
child, for a good artist painted it. Your
father never looked in the least like you,
Alexander.''

When Madam Bemis said that she would
gaze up at her son with a perfect assent of
admiration with which she had never gazed
at his father. Her married life had not been
altogether satisfactory to her. Her husband
had been something of a disappointment.
He was very much a Bemis, as was she, and
there had been a constant, wearying echoing
of family traits. "I wish, Addison, when
you lose your temper, you would not lose
it in exactly the same way that I do," she
told her husband once.

The tastes of the two had been so similar
that they gave rise to that curious discord
which may result from harmony. With such
an identity of hereditary tastes, there was at
once a loss of individuality, and a maddening
intensifying of it as in a convex mirror, and
the result was either weariness or a mon-
strous egotism. In the woman's case it
was weariness; in the man's, egotism. The
woman, when her son came, had for the first
time in her life a distinct interest in something outside herself, and yet belonging to

her. She did not have to admire or dislike in the child her own appearance and traits, or her husband's. He was essentially different from both parents, or appeared to be so. Certainly, he differed from them physically. Both Alexander's parents were small, with fair hair, and he was exactly the reverse. Madam Bemis said that he resembled her own father, who had not been a true Bemis, but had inherited from the mother's side. "My father was the first dark Bemis who ever lived, so far as I know," she said, "and he was like my grandmother, who was a Morril, and was said to have Indian blood. Alexander seems more like father than he does like me or his own father." Then Madam Bemis concluded, as she always concluded everything, all her paragraphs of life, with, as it were, a little tail-piece of a look of boundless admiration at Alexander.

Alexander was accustomed to that look, and not on his mother's face alone. Everybody whom he met looked at him in that fashion. He was never at any time particularly elated by it. He merely acquiesced in it as his rightful due, and had done so from the first. Alexander had been a very precocious child, and not in the least slow

"He used to view his small image"

to recognize his own relation to his environments. Long before people thought that he understood, when they talked before his face of his beauty and brilliancy, he was fully alive to the situation.

"Oh, that baby can't understand what we say," one woman replied to another, who remonstrated with her for her outspoken admiration in the presence of the child. "He doesn't know what a beauty he is, do you, darling?"

But Alexander, who could speak few words, and understood many, and who, besides, had as keen an intelligence for variations of voice and expressions of face as a dog, would look at her with his wonderful contemplative black eyes and understand perfectly.

He knew that he was a beautiful, marvellous little boy; that no other child in the village could equal him; and everybody admired him.

He used to view his small image in the mirror with no vanity, but entire comprehension of its beauty. There had really never been such a beautiful child as Alexander in the village, or perhaps in the State. There was something about that noble,

gentle little face lighted with those great
black stars of eyes, and that little figure full
of the touching majesty of innocence and
childhood, which made a woman's heart
ache with love and desire, and a man's with
ambition and desire.

"That boy is going to be something, if he
lives," they said. They repeated his bright
sayings, which were many. He was a talented child. When he went to school he
soon outstripped those of his own age, and
graduated the youngest of his class, and
was ready for college at seventeen.

Madam Bemis went to college with Alexander. She could not bear her beautiful,
noble son to be long out of her sight. The
Bemis place was shut up during the long
terms, and Madam Bemis lived in the college
town, and made a home for Alexander. But
when the morning-glories were in blossom
the two were home again, and Alexander,
resplendent with new clothes, and new stature, and new knowledge, was passing in and
out of the east door, under the trellis, purple,
and rosy, and white with the trumpet-shaped
flowers.

The admiration of Alexander grew and
grew. He was making a brilliant record at

college; he seemed to be moving on an ascendent scale in everything—mind, looks, and attainments. People began to think that he might in time become almost anything: representative, senator, perhaps even President, at least governor of the State. His mother had the fullest faith in it.

"There is no reason why you cannot be anything that you want to be, Alexander," she would say, and Alexander would flash upon her one of his brilliant, contemplative looks, and make no dissent. There was in reality something sublime in the boy's consciousness of his own power. It was completely removed from vanity. It was a simple, ingenuous recognition of the truth.

"Alexander Bemis does think he's awful smart," said one sharp-tongued, dissenting young girl to another, who retorted:

"Well, he *is* awful smart."

"I would rather he didn't know it," said the first.

"Then he wouldn't be bright," said the other.

Alexander was worshipped afar off by the young girls of the village, but he made a sweetheart of none of them until he had graduated from college. He came home laden with honors. He had won prize after prize. He had been mentioned in the newspapers. Madam Bemis was so proud of him that life was to her like a triumphal march. If the church-bell in this little New England village, which never rang in the interest of any individual, unless his house was on fire or he was on his way to his tomb, had pealed for joy when Alexander came home from college, she would have considered it quite appropriate. What demonstration in greeting of such magnificent promise as that of her son could be out of place?

However, although the bell was not rung, Alexander was made much of in his native village. Young as he was, he was elected a member of the school committee, and was made chairman of the selectmen. At every public meeting he was called upon as "our talented and promising young townsman" to speak. He sat upon the platform with the local dignitaries; his name, prinked out with laudatory adjectives, appeared often in the local paper. Alexander at that time could scarcely sit down, or stand up, or eat his breakfast but it was made the subject of admiring chronicle. He could not speak without a listening hush. He held undisputed moral sway over the whole village, but his head was not in the least turned. He bore all his honors with the magnificent ease and unconcern of one born to a crown.

The year after Alexander graduated Amanda Doane came to live in the village. Her father was a rich manufacturer, who bought out the little factory, and established a gigantic plant, which might in time convert the small town into a city. His daughter was a beauty of a coarse, emphatic type. Not a line wavered, not a color was indeterminate. Her loud, clear voice never faltered in the expression of her opinions. Alexander lost his heart to her at once. The village people quite approved of the match, but Madam Bemis hesitated. For the first time a doubt as to whether the king could not do wrong seized her. When her son told her of his engagement, she looked at him uncertainly.

"Why, what is the matter, mother?" Alexander asked, with wonder.

"She is not like the women of our family," Madam Bemis replied, falteringly.

Alexander laughed. "She is a lady at heart," he replied, "and as for the rest, she

P   225

can acquire it. Not that I am not entirely satisfied," he added, generously.

But Amanda Doane acquired nothing. She remained a fact, settled and incontrovertible. Her period for receptivity had passed. Although she was still young, her character had formed and developed to a perfect flower of resistance to all outside influence.

The engagement was not to be a long one; the wedding-day was set. Then one afternoon Amanda appeared at the Bemis house. Such was her almost brutal directness of action when her mind had once formed a purpose, that she came, rather than send for Alexander. "I don't care if you stay in the room," said she to Madam Bemis; "I would just as soon you heard."

Then she confronted the two, the splendid young fellow and his adoring mother, and made her little speech, which was full of revolutionary eloquence. It was the revolt of a daughter of the people—of the modern conditions of things against all inactive superiority. The girl did not speak good English, but she spoke with a force which made her own language. "Now, you look at here, Alexander Bemis," said she. "I've promised to marry you, and I'm most ready, clothes all bought an' everything. I don't know what you will say, an' I don't know what folks will say, and I can't help it, and I don't care. I'm goin' to back out. I've got to look out for myself, and my father's money, that he's worked so hard to get, without a dollar to start with. I'm goin' to back out. I've liked you, an' I like you now, an' it ain't none too easy for me, an' I've laid awake some nights thinkin' of it, but it's better for both of us. I ain't goin' to marry you. You're good and steady and handsome, and you're awful smart, but you ain't done anythin' but talk smart, an' look smart, an' be smart; you ain't never acted smart, an' I don't believe you ever will. You haven't done anythin'. You've jest laid right back on your reputation, an' that's what you're goin' to do right along. I'd rather have a man with less smartness than you that can use what little he's got. There's no use. I'm goin' to back out."

The girl's voice broke a little; there were tears in her indignant blue eyes; her red lips pouted into sobs, which she resolutely restrained. Alexander towered over her, pale and magnificent and quite silent. His mother shrank into a little, faintly breathing, wide-eyed heap in a corner of a sofa. Amanda pulled the engagement ring, a little ancient pearl hoop, an heirloom in the Bemis family, from her finger.

"Here," said she—"here's your ring. I'll always wish you well."

Alexander took the ring between a long thumb and forefinger—Amanda's were short and stubbed—and looked at it, then at the girl, with a sort of pained and stately acquiescence. "Very well, Amanda," he replied, quite calmly, but his lips were white. Gentleman born and bred, diametrically different by nature and training, he had been very fond of this girl, who defied, with her coarse but splendid vigor, all laws and rules of growth and advance to which she did not herself subscribe.

"Why ain't the kind of English I speak as good as yours?" she had demanded of him once. They would always have spoken two languages had they lived together for a lifetime, but that had not seemed of much moment to him. She had, perhaps, supplied some inherent need of his nature, and been to him a sort of spiritual trellis-work, which had been essential for his future growth.

Be that as it may, after Amanda Doane deserted him he retrograded further and still further from his early promise, though that might have happened in any case.

Amanda soon married a young manufacturer, who went into business with her father. Alexander used often to see her driving in her smart trap, with her keen-looking, alert husband by her side. Later on he saw her with a small brood of children, who were the children of her time as well, who raised a shrill babel of voices, like a multiple of their mother's.

As time went on, and Alexander did no more than he had done, people began gradually to lose faith in him, especially after his mother died. Her faith had served as a prop for that of others. Then slowly Alexander dropped and sagged away from his high estate until he lay nearly prone in his path of life, yet still, even there, with a certain unconquerable beauty and glory. No man could ever say aught against Alexander Bemis, except that he had never done that which he had bade fair to do, and had failed to keep his promise to himself. He lived to be an old man, old and shrunken, going in and out his east door, under the garlands of morning-glories, and people, seeing him, used to speak in this wise: "That is Alexander Bemis. Everybody used to think he was going to be something great, but he never amounted to anything at all. He has never done anything. He used to speak in town-meeting; we thought he would be a Daniel Webster or a Charles Sumner, and go to Congress, but he never did. When he was young everybody thought there was nobody like him in town, but he never came to anything."

Every spring the morning-glories came again and sent forth their great silent chorus of youth and victory from their hundred trumpet mouths. Then at noon they closed and slept, and remained asleep until the next morning, when they awoke again to their chorus of victory, and Alexander passed beneath them, still old and wrecked and defeated. But the day of a man is longer than that of a flower.

THE END